spark

NAOKI MATAYOSHI is a Japanese manzai comedian and author, who found fame performing as part of the popular comedy duo Peace. *Spark* is his first novel and has been a phenomenon in Japan since it was first published in 2015. It has won Japan's most prestigious literary award, the Akutagawa Prize, sold millions of copies and been adapted for film, stage and TV – the hit series is available now on Netflix. The book is publishing in English for the first time.

ALISON WATTS was born in South Australia but has lived long-term in Japan where she is based in Ibaraki prefecture. She has translated novels by Durian Sukegawa and Riku Onda, as well as travel memoirs, and writes about traditional sashiko stitching.

Naoki
Matayoshi

spark

TRANSLATED FROM THE JAPANESE BY ALISON WATTS

Pushkin Press

Pushkin Press
71–75 Shelton Street
London WC2H 9JQ

Copyright © 2015 Yoshimoto Creative Agency Co. Ltd

English translation copyright © 2020 by Alison Watts

Spark was originally published in Japanese as *Hibana*
by Bungeishunju Ltd, Japan in 2015.

World English translation rights reserved by Pushkin Press, under the
licence granted by Yoshimoto Creative Agency Co. Ltd, arranged with
Bungeishunju Ltd, Japan through Japan UNI Agency, Inc., Japan.

First published by Pushkin Press in 2020

ISBN 13: 978-1-78227-590-9

Designed and typeset by Tetragon, London
Printed and bound in the United States

www.pushkinpress.com

3 5 7 9 8 6 4 2

SPARK

THE PIERCING TRILL of bamboo flutes soared over the beat of the drums, and as the heat of the midday sun dissipated into the evening air, the festive crowd, in cotton kimonos and geta, streamed along the road by the bay of Atami.

Yamashita and I—two halves of a *manzai* stand-up comedy duo—were on a tiny makeshift stage, going through our routine. We were supposed to be entertaining the crowds on their way to the fireworks, but the microphone set-up got in the way of the quick-draw banter, forcing us to take turns and bring our faces so close to the mic we looked like we were about to cram it into our mouths. No one really cared—our so-called audience kept walking by, barely noticing us, their laughter for sure not having anything to do with us. It was depressing. And it didn't help that the music was so loud we couldn't be heard from more than a few metres away, which meant we had to say something hilarious every three seconds or end up looking like a couple of dopes just standing there. Not much we could do under those conditions, so reluctantly we were just sort of going through our paces, using up our time.

I can't remember the gags we tried that day, but Yamashita started off with something like: "What kind of thing would you hate to hear your parakeet say?" and I responded, "Be sure to make your pension contributions regularly, however small, it's all about accumulation." Then I came up with a list of things that your average parakeet would *not* be likely to say, like: "You *still* haven't done anything about that wasted space in our apartment," "We need to have a serious talk," "What's with all the strange looks—you're not thinking of eating me, are you?" and "Can we discuss fully what's troubling you?" Yamashita responded to each with a grunt or a quip, but for some reason he thought "Can we discuss fully what's troubling you?" was hysterical and he couldn't stop laughing. He laughed so hard he was gulping for air. His laughter saved me. Gave me a moment to picture myself coming home, feeling good about the day, and the parakeet saying, "Can we discuss fully what's troubling you?" And I'd say, "Yes, but first,

I'm going to take my lighter and singe your pretty little wings." Oh, maybe that would be cruel. Better if I just singed the hair on my arm and scared the bejeezus out of the parakeet. Blow the parakeet's tiny mind! This made me snigger. Truth is, if a parakeet, or anybody else for that matter, had asked me "Can we discuss fully what's troubling you?", right then and there onstage I would have broken down in tears. I felt alienated, it was that lonely, standing there trying to make funny in front of a crowd that didn't care if you existed or not. Suddenly, there was a *BOOM*, and a burst of explosions behind us, coming from the direction of the sea and echoing off the mountains.

The crowd stopped in their tracks and looked up, their faces reflecting red, blue and green. I spun around to see a carpet of lights roll out like a vision in the night sky, then slowly dissolve in a shower of glitter. Before the spontaneous cheering had died away, another firework unfolded in the shape of a gigantic weeping willow, dangling its glowing branches in the darkness. Smaller fireworks spiralled around feverishly, lighting up the night as they fell into the sea. The crowd roared. These fireworks were more beautiful and magnificent than anything else man-made in this city where the surrounding mountains and sea made nature feel close. It was a perfect setting. I wondered now why we'd even been invited here. We weren't really needed.

By now our voices were completely drowned out by the fireworks exploding and echoing off the mountains. I felt small and insignificant, but not despairing, for the very mundane reason that I have tremendous respect for nature and fireworks.

Thinking back, it seems significant that this—a night that brought home my inadequacy in the face of something larger—was also the night when I found my sensei. Saizo Kamiya came along, boldly walked into my life and made himself at home. That was the night I decided to learn from him and no one else.

But back to the manzai stage: driven to desperation by the crowd, which was totally transfixed by the fireworks, I screamed out, in the voice of the parakeet speaking to its owner, "*You're* the parakeet!" And at last our fifteen minutes was up. I was soaked in sweat, feeling zero satisfaction. The plan had been for all entertainment to be finished before the fireworks started, but the guys on before us were a bunch of senior citizens who acted out street theatre and forgot about the schedule once the crowd paid them the least bit of attention, which cut into the time we had before the first fireworks went off. The organizers weren't concerned about trifling programme adjustments at the tail end of the evening either, setting the scene for our tragedy. The fireworks upstaged us and nobody could hear us unless they strained.

When we left the stage, there was still one manzai duo waiting to perform. They emerged less than energetically from the tent—hung with a yellowing banner that read ATAMI JUNIOR CHAMBER OF COMMERCE—where they'd been waiting, and where the senior citizens were now encamped, the beer flowing. As one of the performers brushed past, he turned to me and muttered angrily, "You will be avenged." I didn't understand what he said right away, but now I couldn't take my eyes off him. I slipped into the crowd and watched their act from start to finish. The guy who'd spoken to me was taller than his partner, which forced him to bend over the mic as if he were a dog about to snap at it, all the while glaring angrily at those passing by.

"Thank you, we're the Doofuses," he announced with a scowl, then started in on the crowd as if picking a fight. It's hard to put down everything he said because most of it was unintelligible, but the spit flew as he snarled: "Listen up, my lovelies, I've got the gift. I can tell by looking at you if you're going to hell!" He pointed at people passing by and screamed "hell" at them, in a voice sounding for some reason like a woman's. "Hell, hell, hell, hell, hell, hell, hell, hell, hell, hell, hell—you're all sinners, every one of you. Repent!" And he kept this rant up while his partner—without using the mic—yelled like a demon at anybody who came up to the stage and dared to complain: "I'll kill you, you don't believe me, you come here and see." This chanting and taunting went on until, all of a sudden, the tall guy stopped and went quiet, his eyes fixed on one thing. I looked in the direction his finger was pointing and saw a little girl holding her mother's hand. For a moment my heart missed a beat, and I prayed for him to say nothing. If this was his revenge for us today, I wanted him to stop. But when I turned back to look at him, a big smile was spread across his face. "A fun hell," he whispered in a gentle voice. "Sorry, little girl." I knew then, from that alone, that this guy was the truth.

In the end this duo's performance went down even worse than ours had. The organizer was red-faced with anger as he gave them a dressing-down, but even then the partner never lost the kick-ass look. That was when the tall guy saw me and gave me the sweetest, most innocent smile. It was wide-open purity. I was in awe.

While I was changing in a corner of the tent, the tall guy made his escape from the organizer's tirade and came over to me. "I got paid in cash," he said with a suppressed twitch of the lips. "Wanna go for a drink?"

Fireworks illuminated the hotel-lined streets of Atami as we walked along in silence. He wore a Hawaiian shirt—a tiger against a black background—and faded Levi's 501 jeans on his lean body. His eyes were piercing, and he did not seem very approachable.

We entered a small pub with a weather-worn sign and found a rickety table in the corner. The other customers looked like tired tourists and were mostly older than we were. Everybody seemed to be in a daze after the fireworks show. On the wall was a large square card, autographed by somebody who had to have been famous. The way it was discoloured by tobacco smoke and grease made me think the autographer must be dead.

The tall guy looked at me, his eyes penetrating. "Order anything you like," he said.

There was such kindness in these words that I felt hot with relief. I hadn't realized how intimidated I'd felt until then.

"I should've introduced myself before," I said. "My name's Tokunaga of the Sparks comedy duo."

"I'm Kamiya," he said, "of the Doofuses."

That was how Kamiya and I met. I was twenty at the time so he would have been twenty-four. It was the first time I'd ever been out drinking with a *sempai*, someone senior to me, from the manzai world, and I had no idea what the protocol was, but apparently Kamiya had never gone out drinking with a *kohai*—someone younger, that is, like me—*or* a *sempai* either, for that matter, so we were both new at the game.

"The Doofuses—great name," I said.

"Naming's not my strong point. The old man always used to call me a doofus, so I stuck with it."

The waitress brought a bottle of beer, and for the first time in my life, I performed the ritual of pouring a drink for someone.

"Your duo's got a cool name. And in English, eh? What does your father call you?"

"Father."

Kamiya fixed me in the eye as he raised his glass and emptied it in one gulp, then continued staring straight at me.

"Really," I said a few seconds later, "he calls me Father."

Kamiya's black eyes contracted. "Hey, don't spring the dumbass funny-man act on me," he said. "Took me a while to get that. I couldn't tell if you were joking, or had some complicated family situation, or your old man is an idiot."

"I'm sorry."

"Don't apologize. Always say what comes into your head."

"OK."

"In return, make me laugh. But when I ask a serious question, I want a straight answer."

"OK."

"So I'll ask again. What does your father call you?"

"All you need is love."

"What do you call your father?"

"Ready for the old folks' home?"

"What does your mother call you?"

"I don't know who you take after."

"What do you call your mum?"

"Who *do* I take after?"

"Whoa, those are weird names. But we're getting it together now."

Kamiya leant back in his seat and smiled.

"Not so bad, hey. Since when was it this hard to be funny?"

"I was feeling the pain, too."

"We've still got a way to go. Anyway, let's drink," Kamiya said, pouring for himself since I hadn't mastered the timing for giving him a refill.

I was thrilled at being invited to drink with him and had a string of questions I was dying to ask. "Why," I started off, "did you try to sound like a woman in your routine?"

"Because it's fresh, right," Kamiya said, "and you don't want to be predictable or anything. Any reason I shouldn't sound like a woman?" He looked at me with intensity.

Feeling anxious, as I get when I'm under pressure for a quick answer, I replied earnestly, "Because if people start to wonder why this guy is trying to sound like a woman, maybe it's harder for them to get their heads around the important stuff."

"Did you go to college or something?" Kamiya said uneasily, bringing his face up close to mine.

"High school."

"Idiot, don't make like you're clever when you didn't even go to college," he said, pretending to knock me on the head with his fist. "You have to do something different from other people."

I don't know where the conversation went from there, but around the time Kamiya was on his fifth glass of *shochu*, his face red and eyes heavy, I found myself bowing and saying, "Please take me on as your apprentice." I wasn't joking—the words had bubbled up from somewhere deep inside me.

"Sure," Kamiya said without hesitation, as the waitress arrived with our next round of drinks. "Hey, can you be our witness?" he said to her. "I just agreed to take on an apprentice."

"Yeah, why not," she answered. Still, the importance of the moment and my great confidence in Kamiya, who acted as though he knew what he was doing even if this was new for him, were not diminished. And that was how our relationship—with him as sensei and me as apprentice—began.

"On one condition, though," Kamiya said with a meaningful air.

"What's that?"

"I want you to remember me. Don't forget about me."

"Are you going to die soon?"

Kamiya kept his eyes on me in a steady gaze, not blinking, and made no reply. I wasn't even sure he had heard me.

"You didn't go to college so your memory might not be any good," he said, coming back to our earlier conversation. "You might forget about me. I want you to watch me up close, write down what I do and say, then write my biography."

"Your biography?"

"Yeah, you write my biography and I give you an initiation into manzai."

I wasn't clear what he meant about me writing his biography. Was this the kind of thing you had to do for a sempai?

The company I worked for was a small entertainment agency. In high school I'd entered an amateur manzai competition and afterwards was approached by a kind-looking man, who turned out to be the president of this company. It had one famous actor on its books, someone who'd been on television ever since I was a kid, and a few others, mainly stage actors, but Yamashita and I were the only comic team in the agency. I had hoped that would be to our advantage, but we didn't get many gigs, and what we did get was almost always a long way out of the city or stints like today.

Ever since I started on this path, I wished I could be around some seasoned manzai comedians to learn the ropes, maybe have someone to look up to. Backstage, at the events where manzai duos from different agencies performed, I was always jealous of the conversations between the younger comics and their sempai. Yamashita and I, who had no real place in the dressing room, kept quiet and tried to make ourselves invisible in the corridors.

"Miss, can we have two more glasses of shochu, please?" Kamiya said to the waitress who had come over to announce that this was our last chance to order.

"Sure. You guys here sightseeing?"

Kamiya sat up straight and answered proudly, "I'm a local god." It was such a weird response that the waitress couldn't help but laugh.

"Do you read books?" he said, now turning back to me.

"No, not much."

Kamiya opened his eyes wide and seemed to be study-ing the graphic design on my T-shirt. Then he shifted his gaze to my face. "You should read," he declared. "You should read because you have to be able to write—to write, you know, my biography."

Was Kamiya actually serious about me writing his life story? If so, I was ready to start reading that instant—even though I wasn't what you'd call a reader. Already, I was feeling his influence. There was something about him that made me want to earn his praise. I wanted him to think well of me.

"I like books," Kamiya said happily, poking at a cro-quette with his chopsticks.

Apparently while his primary school classmates were fighting over Barefoot Gen manga and illustrated animal guides, Kamiya had devoured the life stories of the great men and women.

"They had pictures on the covers and there were a few inside, but mostly it was all writing. You know who Inazo Nitobe is?"

"The guy on the five-thousand-yen note, right?"

"Yeah, he did a lot of things. It's all written down."

"Yeah, I guess so... What'd he do?"

"I forget. But I remember it made a deep impression."

Biographies can be interesting, Kamiya was saying. Big accomplishments look good on paper, but on a personal level many great people were fools. When he was small he'd wanted his own biography to surprise people.

"You know," he said, "you're not much good at talking but I see from your eyes you're taking everything in, so I think you have what it takes to write my biography."

"My dream is to make a living from manzai," I piped up, even though I took what he said as a compliment.

Kamiya laughed at this, then said with a wave of his hand, "Don't be so obvious."

"What do you mean, obvious?"

"If you're a comedian, of course your mission is to be funny, and every act in your life is done with manzai in mind. So everything you do is already part of your manzai routine, right? Manzai's not for people who can think up funny stuff, it's an exposure of people who are honest and pure, who aren't faking it. You can't do manzai just by being clever. Only fools who honestly believe they're genuine fools can make it happen."

Kamiya flicked away the hair that fell into his eyes.

"So, you have to live by going at your ambitions full on. Anyone who says a manzai comic should be this or that won't ever be one. You don't even get better at becoming one by doing it for a long time. That's like dreaming it's going to happen. A real manzai comic, to take an extreme example, is doing manzai even if he's selling vegetables."

Kamiya was speaking as if checking each sentence with himself first. It was like he wasn't used to saying this stuff out loud, and maybe it was the first time he'd ever said it to anyone.

"So if I talk about becoming a manzai comedian, I won't become one?" I cautiously asked the question that had been on my mind for a while.

"If you're saying that to try and trip me up, as your sensei I'll kick your ass."

"No, no, I'm just asking, honest," I said quickly. "I really want to know."

Kamiya folded his arms and nodded once. "There's a big difference between saying what a manzai comedian is supposed to be, and talking about manzai comedians. What I'm doing is talking about manzai comedians."

"OK."

"You have to give credit to someone who prepares, shows up on time and delivers. But, say there's a person who's a born manzai comedian, but he grows up never knowing it and he goes on to sell quality vegetables like a good citizen—someone like that is a genuine dumbass funny man. Then you get someone who's totally aware, who gets up onstage and says, 'Meet my partner who doesn't know he's a natural-born manzai comic, and hasn't noticed because he's an idiot so he's still selling vegetables. Why's he selling vegetables? Because he's a fool.' Now, that's a real straight man's line." Kamiya fell silent for a few moments. "But then—" he started, suddenly broke off, started again, "nobody'd laugh at that. So you have to do it with enough conviction to make children, adults and even the gods laugh. Kabuki—it's just like with kabuki."

I was getting it. You had to perform, like they did in kabuki and Noh theatre, which also had their roots in performing for the gods. Otherwise, when there was no one watching you, like today, why bother?

While we were talking, the other customers had departed, and in their place people who looked like locals were coming in and seating themselves on the raised floor at the back of the pub for a private party.

Kamiya picked up his glass of shochu and drained it in one gulp, then held the glass in the air and began counting down loudly: *ten, nine, eight, seven, six*... When he got to *one*, he drew it out—*oooooone*—until the waitress came over and put two more glasses of shochu down on the table. I picked up the glass in front of me and was about to drink it down, when Kamiya said, smiling, "We're not in a hurry." I looked at him and the thought came to me that even if he wasn't a local god, this man in front of me did seem like some kind of apparition.

"A biography usually comes out after someone dies, right?" I suddenly said, not sure why.

"I think you're going to live longer than me," Kamiya said, his eyes seeming to pierce me.

Whoa, I thought. What's that about?

But then, in an abrupt turnabout, he said cheerfully, "Tell you what. Publish the first volume while I'm alive and the second after I die."

"Then there'll be complaints about when the third part's coming."

"That'll make it interesting, won't it?"

Kamiya picked up the tab lying on the table and stood up. Several times he'd said, "This is my treat," which I took to mean he was really asking me to split the bill, but when I offered, he replied, "Idiot, it's the done thing in the entertainment world for sempai to treat kohai," in such a happy way, I realized he'd been wanting to say it.

Kamiya paid the bill and we gripped hands in a fierce handshake—"like two gorillas," he said. And then he added, "That was heavy shit."

"Thanks for the drinks," I said, and without meeting my eyes, he replied shyly, "Not at all, it was nothing." Nervous as I'd been about drinking with a sempai for the first time, Kamiya might have been feeling the same being around an eager kid. Then, with a final farewell of "I'm going this way, see you again", he raced off into the night.

I replayed something he'd said: "Write down what you saw today, do it while it's fresh." A warm sensation filled my chest. Maybe I was looking forward to writing. Or maybe I was happy at having found someone to share my passion with at last. On the way back to where I was staying, I stopped at a convenience store and bought a notebook and pen. Walking back along the road in the cool sea breeze, I mused over what I would write. There were few people out, the visitors who'd come for the fireworks having settled into their hotels, and I could hear the gentle sound of waves. When I heard a ringing in my ears that sounded like fireworks, I broke into a sprint.

* * *

I didn't see Kamiya again for a long while—he had a big agency getting him work in Osaka, and I was getting gigs in Tokyo. He called me often, though. My mobile would ring at the end of a day during which I hadn't spoken to anyone, and when the name Saizo Kamiya flashed on the screen, my heart would leap. First thing he'd always ask—in a weird falsetto—was where are you, and when I'd say Tokyo, he'd make this regretful *uhhhh*, and then start telling me what was up with him. Then, just as he was warming up, the line would cut off, and a few minutes later a text would arrive saying, *sorry. no power. catch u later.* This happened so frequently it got to be routine.

His smooth, confident patter was a source of frustration for me. I could never speak so easy, so fast. Whenever I tried to explain any of the million thoughts whirling around in my head, the words seemed just beyond reach, and I could never get them out. It got worse when I was around more than one person. Every word, every phrase I heard started me off on a new train of thought, and that mixing with all the other thoughts in my head made me a lost cause. I didn't know what to say or how to say it. Kamiya found this amusing.

"Just speak fast. The faster you speak, the more stuff you can get out. The more bats you get at the plate the better, right? Sure it's better to speak fast. But you can't do that, can you? Never mind, there's things you can say that nobody else can. Yeah, you're lucky." My deprived background, he said, was my ticket to creativity. "I had all the usual toys and games, but you had to figure out how to have fun on your own with your family being so poor and all." I could have taken that the wrong way, but Kamiya said it in a way that wasn't mean.

"I'm jealous, man. The kind of stuff you guys made up," he told me. Well, it was true my family didn't have a lot of money. And my sister and I didn't have any toys at all. Sometimes we would spend a whole day just drawing pictures. Other times we would spread out Dad's *shogi* board and make up moves for all the pieces, planning complicated defences for the king in case of attack—and then wait and wait until we figured out nobody was coming to attack. Kamiya, for some reason, thought that was sweet.

Then there was this other story that he liked to hear me tell over and over. My sister was learning the piano, and because we didn't have a piano or electric keyboard like her friends did, she used to practise "Chopsticks" and stuff on a keyboard made out of paper, humming the notes as she played them. One day after my mother picked me up from daycare, we went to the Yamaha class to see my sister play. When we got there, the students were playing together, all except for my sister, who was looking panicked and sort of pounding on the keys here and there. What was wrong? Why wasn't she playing the song? When she told the teacher that the keyboard didn't have any sound, the teacher leant over and hit the power switch. That was all, but it left my sister stiff and defeated with her shoulders hunched up. It really hurt seeing my kind, dependable big sister like that, and I started to cry.

"Stop," my mother said. "She's doing her best." But I could see that her eyes were red too.

At home later, my sister didn't say anything about what had happened. She just went back to her paper keyboard and practised like she always did, so I sat next to her and hummed along loudly to whatever she was supposed to be playing. Our father, who'd been drinking, yelled at us to stop making noise, but we didn't stop. A week later, a small, beautiful upright piano was delivered to our tiny prefab house. It was a big surprise for my sister, but our father was not happy—and he shouted at our mother for buying it without consulting him.

Kamiya loved this story. It seemed to warm his heart, and he'd sniff and say, "Oh, that's nice. With a background like that, there's got to be stories only you can come up with."

*   *   *

After the fireworks in Atami, a year went by with nothing much changing in Kamiya's career or mine. Meanwhile, a few of our contemporaries—the showy smooth-talkers— were getting on television. I wasn't so thick as to blame the economy for my lack of success. I knew there was a glaring gap between my talent and theirs.

Since our agencies didn't bring in enough work, to earn a spot in TV or stage productions we had to prove our stuff in the auditions held monthly in small theatres. Late at night I would join the crowd of young comedians crammed into tiny waiting rooms, hungry and grubby but with our eyes shining. It was a surreal scene, and far from glamorous. Each duo performed their routine in front of production writers who were in charge of the live shows. After a long day, it couldn't have been easy for them either. I sometimes wondered if tiredness ever clouded their judgement. You can tell when someone is physically exhausted because they collapse, but with the brain it's not so obvious. Still, nobody complained. There was an unspoken rule that you had to earn the right to say what you wanted, and if you didn't succeed in the auditions, you kept your opinions to yourself. Nobody enforced this rule with us, but we all followed it. Each of us fought for a spot on the stage, for the right to express ourselves and maybe for an escape from poverty.

Sparks finally scored a couple of appearances at theatres—was that ever nice. Once that happened we got invited to live shows produced by other agencies, and then we got mentioned in magazines as new faces in comedy, and little by little audiences began to remember us.

Then I heard from Kamiya that he was planning to move to Tokyo. He'd been in the business six years now and felt he'd reached his limits in Osaka. Many of his contemporaries there were getting opportunities in television programmes, and those who didn't were quitting. Kamiya was tired of being the old man among all the young guys in the theatres. The ideal career path was to make a name for yourself in Osaka first, then go to Tokyo, but it wasn't uncommon for those who fell through the cracks of the theatre system to move to Tokyo and make a new start there. Tokyo wasn't easier, but some manzai duos managed to break through there. It was also true that a select few would do well anywhere.

The agencies all preferred obedient young comedians over older guys with chequered histories. Kamiya's artistic sense was—even for me, his apprentice—unsettling. Distinctive, but unsettling. And he was clumsy in his interpersonal skills too. Both members of the Doofuses were. They may not have been well known to the general public, but among entertainers they were notorious. By most social standards, the Doofuses were a couple of complete idiots. Kamiya's partner, Obayashi, had the reputation of being a hood, but typical of tough guys, he was also soft-hearted. Violence—or a threat of violence—was his only defence against spite. Kamiya was a little like that too—hard-edged and scary on the surface but a different person on the inside.

So when I heard Kamiya was coming to Tokyo, I couldn't be sure if what I felt was happy anticipation, or apprehension.

*   *   *

One morning in autumn, I was walking in my neighbourhood, looking for the sweet osmanthus tree whose scent had filled the air during the night. The young guy I usually saw pimping for customers outside the oral sex café went by on his bicycle. Just as I approached the main drag and decided to turn back, a text arrived from Kamiya: *will live in kichijoji. where r u? peaches everywhere.* Immediately I replied: *Koenji. On my way to Kichijoji now. Weeping osmanthus.* I ran to the station, dashed up the stairs to the platform and jumped on the Sobu Line train before I could calm down. He was here! As the train carried me along to Kichijoji, I looked out the window down on a city tinged by fall colours.

The north exit of Kichijoji Station on a Saturday afternoon was packed with students and family groups. I spotted Kamiya standing amidst the river of people streaming toward their respective destinations, with a serious expression on his face and cloaked in an air of heaviness, as if all gravity in the vicinity was concentrated on his shoulders. In this everyday setting, he was a bundle of awkwardness.

When he noticed me, he broke into a broad smile. "I thought it was some strange ghost coming at me, but then I saw it was you," he said.

"Don't steal my line. Get outa here. Go back to Osaka," I laughed.

As we walked together, Kamiya launched enthusiastically into a monologue on why autumn feels so melancholic. It's because getting through winter used to be a life-and-death struggle for humans, just as it was for animals, and many people didn't make it, so the heaviness we feel in autumn is a hangover of the fear of a killing winter. That was logical enough, but I couldn't really get into it.

"Aren't you impressed?... Nothing to say?"

Kamiya's question jerked me back. "Oh, sorry."

"Nah, don't apologize. I was looking forward to telling you this stuff, getting some respect, you know, ever since the bus left Osaka."

Kamiya was never one to be embarrassed about revealing what he really hoped or feared. It was one of the things I liked about him. And it disarmed me. "Well, you see," I started, "I feel down all year round. Maybe my ancestors were in permanent danger?"

"Could be. But maybe if they'd lived somewhere with

no danger at all, they'd find something else to make them nervous," Kamiya rattled off in quick reply.

"If that's true, they were sorta dumb."

"Yeah, well, who knows."

We set out walking aimlessly for a couple of hours around town, then at some point found ourselves part of the stream of people heading for Inokashira Park.

Wind blew through the autumn leaves on the trees and bushes, brushing our cheeks as we made our way down the stairs. Time seemed to flow more slowly, and Kamiya blended in at last with all the people wandering and mingling. I had a special thing for the park at twilight and was happy Kamiya was here to experience it with me.

Alongside the lake, a young guy had set up his things and was beating a long, narrow drum. His expression was dull and listless, and he played that way too. There was something about him that bugged me, but Kamiya lost no time before he went and planted himself right in front of the guy, standing there looking at him and at the instrument in turn. The musician stopped playing, unnerved by the attention, and looked up, frowning.

"Come on, do it properly!" Kamiya yelled.

Which shocked me. Kamiya was scowling at the guy, eyes wide. The musician froze for a moment, touched the brim of his red cap, then looked down in embarrassment, a movement that suggested he didn't want to believe this was happening.

But Kamiya wouldn't let him off the hook. "Hey, I'm talking to you!"

I wondered if Kamiya had lost his head in that moment. I thought about intervening. But I was also curious where this was all going.

"Look, you're supposed to be *performing*—right? If you don't want anybody to hear you, do it at home. No big deal. But if you're gonna do it outside, and along I come, and I've never seen an instrument like that before... Think about it. It's freaking cool, man, that drum. I wanna know what kind of sound it makes. Get it? Come on, don't be a lazy bastard, give us something to listen to."

The guy looked up at Kamiya. "It's not that kind of thing," he said sullenly.

"Not what kind of thing?" Kamiya turned and looked at me uneasily. "You think I'm being some kind of jerk?"

"Yup, total jerk," I said, laughing. Which Kamiya didn't seem to appreciate.

Anyway, I apologized to the guy and said we'd move on soon but could he play some more first. Reluctantly, he began beating on the long, narrow drum. Kamiya stood there with eyes closed and arms crossed, tapping out the rhythm with his right foot. Relieved, the guy upped the tempo a bit. People looked at us curiously as they passed by. The guy was putting more energy into his playing now. He raised the tempo even more and began a kind of drum roll. Kamiya, still keeping rhythm with his right foot, put out his right hand, palm open, and pushed against the air twice. In response the drummer reined in the beat, bringing it down to a level that seemed to satisfy Kamiya. The guy kept a tight rhythm as he lost himself in the performance again. Several young women gathered round to watch and listen. Seeing an audience, the guy broke into a funky rhythm, whereupon Kamiya once again raised his hand to bring the performance under control, all the while keeping time with his foot. The drummer broke off the funk and went back to his previous style. Kamiya was conducting this scene! Sweat ran down the drummer's face and the crowd around us grew, my head nodding, unconsciously beating time, as an echo of the beats lingered and merged into a kind of melody, one of which Kamiya was an integral part. The drummer shook his long hair under the red cap, still lost in his drumming.

And then, abruptly, Kamiya burst loudly into song—a nonsense kind of chant: "Drum-drum, drummer boy! Drum-drum, drummer boy! Drummer boy in a red cap!

Wake up, dragon! To the beat of the drum!" I tried to shush him, but nothing could stop him now.

Drops of rain began to fall in the deepening violet dusk. The crowd took this as a sign to disperse, but the young man continued beating his drum, oblivious. When the rain grew heavy, Kamiya, the conductor and lead singer of this chaos, and I dashed off. Rain was bouncing off the road by the time we caught sight of a sign for the Musashino Coffee Shop.

Opening the door to the café, we were met with a warm glow from light fixtures on white walls and classical music playing quietly in the background. It seemed like a dream after the noise and confusion we had just left. We sat down next to the window and watched as people scurried towards the station.

I asked for a blended coffee, and Kamiya wanted just a slice of cheesecake, but when he was told that he needed to have a cup of coffee since this was a speciality coffee shop, Kamiya with surprising meekness ordered a cup of Jamaican Blue Mountain, the most expensive on the menu. "Cool policy," he said. "I'd be pissed if someone asked me to sing instead of hearing comedy."

In these pleasant surroundings, it was fun to sip our coffee and laugh about the feverish scene in the park a short while before.

That then led Kamiya to start philosophizing: "The essential thing, Tokunaga, is to disrupt things. Disrupt the colourful, beautiful world, and another unreal, more awesomely beautiful world will appear all on its own. That dude in the park had a radical instrument, but he wasn't doing anything with it. An instrument like that has to be taken seriously. There's no beauty in a world where it isn't. I dunno how he got that instrument, but somehow he did, so now he owes it to the world to play the hell out of it. You can't just go through the motions—it has to be done with total heart." And then he sipped his very expensive coffee.

"Drum-drum, drummer boy! Drummer boy in a red cap," Kamiya muttered huskily. His voice was sounding hoarse from all the shouting.

"But c'mon—'Wake up, dragon! To the beat of the drum!' That's pretty lame," I said. "And the rhyme is wrong."

"Dragons always had it too good. They're so cool it stinks. Extreme is good. Oversized is funny too. Excess in everything is good. You have to be extreme and take the rap for it," he said, sipping more coffee. He didn't take milk or sugar with his, so I, too, was drinking an unfamiliar bitter coffee straight.

"But that stuff about taking the rap is already overdone, don't you think? Such a cliché," I said after a bit. Somehow I could say things like that to Kamiya.

He looked thoughtful for a while. The sound of cups clinking in their saucers echoed through the shop. "That's the difficult part, to be honest. Just because it's a cliché doesn't mean there's not some pure coolness to it."

"What's that mean?"

"Well, the stuff about having to take the rap—sure, I've heard that before, but that doesn't mean I have to reject that idea. Why should I—because it's ordinary? You can't go round rejecting stuff because it's ordinary, you gotta decide whether stuff is OK as a kind of measure to live by."

Suddenly we were talking—getting to the root of things. Kamiya's manzai used the familiar to wreak havoc, so was this why he did it?

"If you judge ideas by how ordinary they are, then creativity just turns into a contest of who or what's the most unusual. On the other hand, if you reject new, unusual stuff completely from the outset, then it's just a contest of technique. But if it's only a combination of technique and originality that gets approved, then it turns into a contest who can be the most balanced."

"Yeah, I think that's right," I agreed without reservation.

"So if you try to measure everything by just one standard, you get blinded. Like those acts who only care about getting the audience on their side—don't you think that's creepy? Sure, it's nice, but when getting the audience's sympathy is the main aim of your act, there's no chance of anything awesomely interesting coming out of it. You can't always go for obvious stuff that pleases everyone and that even idiots understand—anyone in the creative life has to graduate from that stage. Otherwise you'll never be able to see anything else at all. At least, that's my principle," Kamiya said slowly, enunciating every word.

"Critique is difficult, though."

"Yeah, it's hard to do logically. A new critical methodology comes along and attracts all these followers. They develop it some more, refine it; meanwhile others declare it just the latest fad. They're usually the type getting on in years, which gives them authority, makes them convincing. So that methodology is now regarded as wrong. And even if it might be a necessary form of expression in certain cases, people choose not to use it. New ideas are stimulating and people get off on feeling good about them. But in the end if they're undeveloped, abandoned before they mature, it's a helluva waste. If you only ever go for the feel-good buzz of the latest thing, that's like breaking off a branch that's just started to grow. That's why fields full of mean-ass critics fall into decline. Better to stick with the thing until you nail it, and it's matured. Until that method of expression becomes a well-developed branch of a big tree. A lot of stuff'd be more interesting then. What's with all this talk of cutting off branches to let the trunk grow? Yeah, sure, that might be one way, but then you can't see the whole thing from afar, and it won't bear fruit. I promise you this—if you ever get into the game of being a critic, you won't have the ability to do manzai any more."

I wanted to say his speech sounded like a critique of society, but held back from comment. There was truth in what he said, even though, to my way of thinking, it couldn't apply to everyone. Rejecting hard-to-understand new styles in order to protect a particular field was legitimate self-defence in my opinion. All being equal, however, Kamiya's way of thinking was more interesting. But it was a gamble.

What I did say was this: "But I don't think I can avoid passing judgement."

Kamiya held the coffee cup in his hand without moving, eyes wide open. A familiar song played quietly in the background, repeating the same words over and over. What was it called?

"That's right. That's why the only way is to be a fool, no? Be honest in judging according to your own sense of what's interesting. And don't be swayed by other people's opinions. If I ever start putting down other people's work all the time, please kill me. I wanna stay a manzai comedian forever." Kamiya paused to examine the surface of his drink. "This coffee's good."

"Yeah, it's good. But listen, it's OK to, like, have empathy for the sensibility of your teacher, right?"

"That's what we're doing now..." Kamiya said, looking self-conscious. "Being *empathetic*."

I guessed he was embarrassed about being led by me into using a word he wouldn't use ordinarily. But that was an instinct in him I felt I could also trust. He might sound contradictory, but I was more afraid of clever people who threw the latest words around with ease.

"Hey, did you notice whenever I put my cup in the saucer I wasn't making any noise?" he said.

"Yeah, actually I did."

"Why didn't you say something? How could I find the right time to stop doing it while you still hadn't said anything?" His voice sounded husky.

As we were leaving the coffee shop, the owner offered us a plastic umbrella. "I've only got one, sorry, but there's no need to return it."

Kamiya was moved by this kindness and thanked the owner profusely. Outside, it was hardly raining enough to require an umbrella, but Kamiya opened it anyway and set off. I pulled my umbrella out of my bag, opened it and hurried to catch up with Kamiya. Beyond the drifting high clouds, the sky was darkening. Car lights and street lights cast sparkling reflections on the wet roads. The rain soon stopped completely.

"Number eighty-two!" Kamiya suddenly burst out.

It made no sense whatsoever, but hearing him say it made me happy. Here was another person in the world who spontaneously came out with meaningless utterances—I was not alone in this.

"Drum-drum, drummer boy! Drummer boy in a red cap! Wake up, dragon! To the beat of the drum." I don't know who started first, but we both began singing the crazy song Kamiya had made up in the park. As we walked along the streets that smelt of freshly fallen rain, with the moon peeking through the clouds, the town at dusk was luminous and bright, and moving through it all were people coming and going. Only Kamiya and I had our umbrellas open. Nobody gave us a second look. Kamiya made no attempt to explain why he still had his umbrella open, but several times he looked up at the sky and said, "What timing, eh? What is it with the rain stopping?" and looked at me as if in commiseration. He felt a need to do justice to the thoughtfulness of the coffee-shop owner's offer. I completely understood. At the same time, I felt a mixture of admiration, envy and even disdain for the undoubting sincerity of his conviction that holding open the umbrella—when it wasn't raining—was the best way to express that emotion, but I loved that in him, even as it scared me.

*   *   *

The end of the year. Everyone on the streets in dark clothing, rushing about. Kichijoji was full of life as usual, but the noise of the city felt muffled, indistinct, as if played through a radio speaker. Perhaps the chilly air was affecting my eardrums.

Outside the north exit of the station, enormous Christmas and New Year decorations lit the area brightly.

"Guess they haven't finished putting things up," Kamiya said. "Can't wait to see how it turns out."

He must not have been familiar with the geometric style of this year's illuminations, because things were finished; that was the look, but I wasn't sure if I should tell Kamiya that.

Kamiya and I had been hanging out in Kichijoji, going there practically every day as if we were taking measurements. We'd wander about until we got tired and then head to Mifune, a dive in Harmonica Alley, for a couple of drinks and a plate of fried pork and garlic stems. Then we'd move on to whatever other cheap pub we could find. By the time we were ready to call it a night, the trains had stopped running. Kamiya would always say, "Stay over at my place," since it was near. I would always say, "Nah, no need, thanks." I didn't think it was a great idea to pass out drunkenly in front of a sempai, so if I had a bit of money to spare, I'd stay in a manga café, and if I didn't, I'd sleep on a bench in Inokashira Park until the trains started running again.

Tonight, blind drunk once again, Kamiya invited me to stay over. I shook my head. "I feel five times sicker than if I was on a boat."

But he wouldn't let me go. "What a piss poor line. I'm worried about you, man. You need training," he said, grabbing my arm. "C'mon, you're going to my place." And with that he attempted to pull me along by force. I was on the verge of vomiting, and Kamiya wasn't so steady himself.

"Let me go," I said, shaking his hand from me, still determined to go off by myself.

Out of the blue, Kamiya wound up and kicked me in the butt. *Thwack.* The sound echoed through the nearly empty streets. A homeless guy turned to look in our direction.

"Man, why'd you do that? That hurt!"

Kamiya fell to his knees, laughing. "Don't be mad. I'm just worried 'cause you're drunk. C'mon on, let's go." He walked off, the so-called explanation hanging in the air behind him.

I gave up and followed, my throat burning, trying to keep the vomit down. We walked and walked and walked, but still didn't reach Kamiya's apartment. I was starting to think this was another of his crazy tricks, but every now and then he'd turn around to ask, with disarming concern, "Are you OK, Tokunaga?" So I thought it couldn't be a joke. We walked along Kichijoji Avenue for an eternity. By the time we passed Nerima Tateno post office, the sky was getting light in the east. I still felt queasy, and now the sight of Kamiya leisurely parading down the middle of the street made me furious.

"How far is it? We're not in Kichijoji any more."

"Aww, don't get upset now. You'll make me sad," Kamiya said, looking at me reproachfully.

"How come you're suddenly talking normal?"

"What do you mean? Please don't be mad at me." For punctuation, he made a scared face.

"Please don't act normal."

"Like what?" he said, innocently puzzled, raising his eyebrows.

"You know what I mean."

"Gee, don't talk like that. You really will make me sad." This time he made a frown.

"I'm the only one who knows that when you pretend to act normal, you're being dumbass funny."

"Don't talk like that," he said. Worried face this time.

"Say something weird, will you!"

"Tokunaga, you make me sad talking like that."

Every time he spoke he'd stop and turn around deliberately so I could see his face.

"If saying normal stuff is a dumbass joke, you're hilarious pretty much all the time," I said.

"You can't go round talking about people like that." Kamiya drew his eyebrows together sternly.

The way he did it enraged me. "May I vomit?" I spat.

"You wouldn't like it if you found a pile of vomit outside your house in the morning when you came out to go to work. It's not a good idea to do something you wouldn't like other people doing to you."

Again, more normal stuff. Though, come to think of it, this stubborn persistence was also pure Kamiya.

"OK, OK. Just *please* stop talking normal. It's too weird."

Kamiya had been punching numbers into his mobile phone as he walked, but now it rang. "Hi, we'll be there soon. Can you buy some water? He's really drunk," he said and hung up.

We walked and walked and walked—this after we were supposed to be there "soon"—when, at last, the sky so bright I couldn't look at it, we came to a major road. The Ome Highway. We cut across, dodging trucks barrelling along, and entered a residential area, then walked some more, east, along a fairly wide road until we reached a shopping strip with the banner Fujimi Street. It was well and truly morning by now. Still he made me walk. Somewhere along the way Fujimi Street became Chuo Street, then finally we got to a building with a rotary out front and a sign that read "Seibu Railway, Kami-Shakujii Station". For sure, we were not in Kichijoji any more.

"We're here," Kamiya said, pointing to an old apartment building that was a lot classier than I'd been expecting.

We climbed the stairs to the second floor where Kamiya stuck a key into an apartment door. Through the doorway I saw a woman sitting on a futon that looked as if it might be kept out permanently in the middle of the floor.

"Yo, give Tokunaga here some water," Kamiya said, leaping on to the futon with a thud.

"Quiet, it's still early. The neighbours'll complain," the woman chided gently. She was slender and had on fashionable striped sweat pants.

"Hi, I'm Tokunaga," I said to her.

"I'm Maki," she said softly, and smiled.

"Sleep!" Kamiya ordered, slapping the futon, then popping up.

The moment I lay down my head felt like it was cracking open. I shut my eyes.

"I'm going to the convenience store. Want anything?"

I didn't reply since I wasn't able to speak. Then I heard the door shut and two sets of feet go down the stairs. The room was too bright, and my forehead itched. Was that woman Kamiya's girlfriend? Maybe this wasn't his apartment after all. Maybe it was hers, maybe he was just staying here.

I lay there awake, head splitting. I knew I wouldn't sleep well here and wanted to go home, sleep in my own futon. I could if I could move. The trains were running now. If only I could get up and move. Why did I let this happen to me?

I always ended up in a heap after a night out with Kamiya. We hardly ever had any worthwhile discussion either. Like today, we'd spent long hours seriously debating who you'd need on a team to pull off the perfect murder, supposing you already had a magician and a strongman on board. Kamiya said Golgo 13, the manga hit man. I said someone with a death wish. Golgo would almost certainly succeed in the mission, but you'd have to pay him a huge amount of money, and getting all that money together would alert the authorities. So, it wasn't foolproof. Someone who wanted to die, on the other hand, would want the same thing as the other two, and you'd be able to compose the perfect farewell note. Kamiya had his doubts about this: someone who was looking to commit suicide was capable of only killing himself, and besides, you wouldn't want your team to kill just anyone. You'd want your killers to kill bad guys. Then Kamiya said that if someone wants to commit suicide, you should try to persuade them not to, which was a just and reasonable point of view, but out of place in our discussion. Once reason and morality got introduced, everything got complicated. I now regretted saying insensitive things about someone having a death wish. Strictly speaking, you shouldn't think about killing anyone, not even a bad evil guy.

Footsteps on the stairs. Maybe someone was coming to kill me. The door opened, but I kept my eyes shut. I heard a plastic bag being placed on the floor.

"He's fast asleep," Kamiya said with a laugh.

I could feel Kamiya's gaze still on me. "He's like an annoying kid brother," he was saying to Maki.

Which made me feel embarrassed.

From the sound of his footsteps, I could tell that Kamiya had jumped over me and gone to the window. His muffled laughter burned my ears. Bright light burned my eyelids, and I could swear an insect was crawling across my forehead.

"Quit that," Maki said.

I slowly opened my eyes to see Kamiya merrily lifting the curtain so that sunlight flickered on my face.

"Stop, please," I begged.

Kamiya would not. "I'm trying to burn your face so you look like Black Jack." He laughed some more.

"What's so funny about that?" I said, covering my face with the blanket.

"Oy, killjoy!" He tore the blanket away and lifted the curtain again.

"Let him sleep," Maki said.

I sat up and swiftly changed ends so that the light wouldn't hit me in the face. Kamiya kept laughing.

Next thing I knew the futon was in the air and I was getting spun around. Kamiya was holding one end of the futon and Maki the other, and they were going round and round.

"Maki, why are you helping him?" I cried.

"Sorry," she said, and put her end of the futon down.

I gave up trying to sleep and sat cross-legged on the futon. In between sips from the bottle of water which Maki gave me, I gazed at motes of dust dancing in the sunlight.

Maki looked at me. "I'm sorry," she said again, and kept smiling.

*　　*　　*

Early in the new year, Kamiya asked me to meet him in Shibuya. This was a surprise, not our usual stomping grounds. The whole of Shibuya seemed to be yelling at the top of its voice, with giant screens on buildings around the station blaring sounds that clashed and merged with the clamour of all the people in the crowd moving about in their own bubbles of sound. People wore fresh, expectant new-year faces even though their bodies were no different from a few days earlier, and while most were dressed in conventional dark clothes, it was the occasional young person in over-bright clothing, laughing to themselves, who made me feel sort of at home. Kamiya was smoking a cigarette as he waited for me by the statue of the famous dog, Hachiko. I was used to how he looked in Kichijoji, but seeing him in the buzzing heart of Shibuya, I was struck anew by how he stood out like a sore thumb, not blending in at all with his surroundings. Maybe it was the way he dressed, his indifference to style or fashion.

"Hey," he said, greeting me as he puffed on a Short Hope cigarette, "Maki says sorry about New Year's."

I guessed he was referring to what happened the last time I was at Maki's place. At New Year's the three of us did the traditional thing and went to the Musashino Hachimangu shrine in Kichijoji, then headed back to Maki's for a kimchi hotpot. I was drunk as usual and going on and on about manzai this and manzai that, when Maki, at Kamiya's direction, made a face at me—crossed her eyes and poked out her tongue—which I told her to quit doing, but she did it again, and I said it again, and we kept this stupid argument up until it totally degenerated, and Maki got up and left, then reappeared to give me the finger.

When the lights at the scramble crossing turned green, Kamiya got rid of his cigarette and we set off. He bumped into other pedestrians a lot. I did too. As we got to the other side, he said, "Tokunaga, I know this isn't your strong point, but we're meeting some girls today."

Apparently we were headed for a pub near the Udagawa police box, where these girls would be waiting for us. The building that housed the pub was a lot more modern than the places where we usually drank in Kichijoji, and I was nervous by the time we put a foot on the stairs leading up. I'd never been at a drinking party with girls before.

Three girls and one of Kamiya's kohai from his agency were waiting for us. The guy hadn't been in the comedy business as long as I had and greeted me politely enough, but I might have come across as unfriendly.

Kamiya was more outgoing that evening than he usually was with Maki and me, while I kept quieter than usual: I couldn't think of a single thing to say that would be appropriate in this company. The girl sitting next to me kept talking into my ear in a really irritating manner.

Kamiya held the stage and the girls laughed at everything he said. Annoyingly, the girl next to me kept whispering, "You OK?" trying to force me into a twosome space with her. The more she did it the more relaxed her eyes looked. But I'd come here to listen to Kamiya, not this girl. I went to the toilet and when I came back, I sat down next to him.

"Hey, where do you think you're sitting!" Kamiya exclaimed.

The girls all laughed. I said nothing and just stared at the plate of cold fried chicken.

"Aww, doesn't he like me?" said the girl I'd been sitting next to.

I stayed silent. Those girls kept looking at me like I was some kind of strange animal. That night I didn't get drunk at all.

"Like a schoolboy, isn't he?" Kamiya asked, and everybody except me nodded in agreement.

Before then I'd been conscious of the huge gulf in talent between Kamiya and myself, but I had never felt so distant from him as a person as I did now. He was like someone from another world. Nevertheless, I knew him better than anyone else there, so I depended on his lead in this situation. But when he said, "He might not look it, but this guy gets off listening in on private moments, you know," I could see the others were shocked. "Don't you?" Kamiya said to me.

"Yes," I answered, and everybody laughed for some reason.

"No kidding, better watch out for him," Kamiya's kohai said, causing the girls to giggle loudly.

It wasn't pervy like Kamiya was making it seem. I didn't use a bug or anything like that. Kamiya was talking about what happened late one night when we were walking along a street and heard some moaning coming from an apartment, so of course we stopped and listened. It was a woman moaning. We listened—for maybe twenty minutes. I went back to the same spot the next night to see if I could hear it again. I did this for a few nights but didn't hear anything. And then I started to think that maybe it wasn't a real woman that first night, maybe the moaning came from a television or video or something. But it sounded real, and the fact that neither of us thought it came from a TV was proof that it wasn't. Once I started doubting I went back for maybe another week because then I wanted to know if it was real or not. That's why I didn't like being referred to as some kind of weirdo who did this for kicks.

"So, apart from the obvious, what's so interesting about listening in?" one of the girls asked a little aggressively.

I didn't want to answer, but I also didn't want to throw cold water on the party. So I said, "Because the individual is projecting sound on the assumption nobody will hear it. As a result, it's something we wouldn't ordinarily hear."

"A scientist!" another girl exclaimed, and everybody laughed.

That didn't bother me. But it hurt that Kamiya seemed to find this funny too and laughed along with the others. If my sensei was taking their side, it was hard for me to dismiss their comments as worthless.

I was a fish out of water that night right to the end. All I wanted was to get out of there, and in answer to my prayers the thing ended before the trains stopped running. Kamiya exchanged contact details with all the girls and then the two of us headed back to Kichijoji on the Inokashira line.

Kamiya was looking very pleased with himself. "You gonna listen in to some more moaning tonight?" he said out of the corner of his mouth.

"Hey, don't bring that up again," I said, not amused, not looking at him.

"Look, if we only talked to each other, we'd be stuck in our own little fantasy world. You have to get out and have conversations with other people sometimes, find out what kind of person you are. We had a good laugh, eh?"

"Nope. I just got laughed at." Suddenly I felt insecure.

"Make 'em laugh, don't get laughed at. Isn't that what they say? That all sounds well and good but that little saying should never've been heard outside backstage," Kamiya said.

At Shimokitazawa a ton of passengers got off, but just as many got on.

"That little bit of wisdom's made it harder to act dumb on purpose to get laughed at. The audience are thinking that guy's playing the fool, but we know he's really smart. Jeez, that's not something they need to know. Now they're judging us by a new standard, when it would've been so much better if they could just laugh at fools without thinking about it. Now they know they're being manipulated into laughing. A real shame they've got so aware—helluva waste."

"But don't new standards spark new kinds of creativity?"

"Yeah, to a degree, I suppose—but if you have a masterpiece and try to touch it up and end up with too much paint on it, you can't go back to the original, so you end up not knowing what to do. As for you, you still haven't figured out why you're so funny," Kamiya said, then paused. "That's good."

"Who's the real fool then?!"

"Keep it down," Kamiya said.

A crowd got off at the Meiji University stop, and at last we had space to breathe. Kamiya was back to his usual self, not like how he'd been in the pub. Which let me relate to him better. Every so often Kamiya would say he worried people would think he was a hypocrite for hanging out with me. At first I took it as a joke, even though there was an element of scorn in what he said. It's hard to be objective about yourself, but thinking about how I acted at the party that night, I could see it might not necessarily be a joke. Those girls'd probably go off and talk about the weird guy they'd met. And Kamiya's kohai was probably thinking how slow-witted I was for a comedian.

Pardon me for talking so much about myself, but people often think I'm cynical—even hostile or aggressive—when the fact is, I come off looking stiff and unapproachable because I'm nervous and insecure. It doesn't mean I'm not interested in people. When I first heard somebody say, half-mockingly, that I did what I wanted and didn't get my hands dirty with other people, I thought, Well, maybe that's what I should do, even though that's not what I had in mind to begin with, and so, little by little, I started talking and acting that way. Then that was taken as proof of what people had been saying—that I was aloof, followed my own path, didn't care about what anybody thought, that sort of thing.

The worst thing, though, was nobody said anything about my talent. Like it wasn't there. I was trying to form myself into a comedian but I didn't have anything solid to stand on; I was so uncertain I didn't know if I was confused, or if that was actually the real me. The long and short though is I was recognized as a real pain in the neck.

Until now I never seriously considered the possibility of people being prejudiced against Kamiya for hanging out with someone as boring and troublesome as me, and calling him a hypocrite for it. I thought Kamiya and I were the same—incapable of playing up to others—but that wasn't so. There was an absolute difference between us: while I would never be able to, Kamiya could but chose not to. Kamiya didn't get defensive with me like other people did, and though he might have made fun of me at times, he also gave me honest praise. He was always straight with me, judging me by nobody else's standards, only his own.

I got used to that. But I was so close to him, and so in awe of his eccentric behaviour and talent, that I was blinded: I got to believing that being abnormal was right, the way to go, the path to take. That might be an asset for comedians, and Kamiya sure was good at it, but me, I was just awkward—so awkward I couldn't capitalize on it, sell it. And somewhere along the line, I'd confused

Kamiya's peculiarity with my own awkwardness. They were not the same. The situation was a lot more serious than I thought.

At Eifukucho, people got off the train, but nobody got on. Cold wind swept through the open doors, wrapping itself around our feet. In our reflection in the windows, our faces looked unearthly.

"Kamiya, are you and Maki, like, an item?" I asked to change the mood, a question that'd been on my mind awhile.

"Nah, she just lets me stay there."

"Oh."

Since first meeting Maki, Kamiya had invited me back to the apartment many times. Often the three of us met at some place to eat and then went back there. Maki was devoted to Kamiya and kind to me as well. She'd crossed my mind repeatedly this evening while we'd been out with those girls. I liked just the three of us going out much better. One reason I liked Maki was because she recognized Kamiya's talent. Watching her when he spoke, I could see she was in love with him from the bottom of her heart.

"I thought she was your girlfriend."

"Did you?" Kamiya replied evenly.

"Don't you like her?"

"Talking with you is like being in school again."

"Well, I'd be in a senior year now if I'd gone to college."

"Wouldn't know about that. But yeah, I don't pay rent, and she does a lot for me so I'd like to do right by her, but it'd be hell for her to be with someone like me."

"Yeah, I guess so."

"You don't have to agree," Kamiya said in a detached voice, looking straight ahead. "If I say I'm meeting you, she always gives me money. That's how I can hang out with you every day."

"But living together like that, don't you ever talk about getting together?"

"Yeah, a few times. I told her to find a proper boyfriend."

Kichijoji, the last stop, was announced over the loud-speakers. The train brakes seemed to screech almost politely as the train slowed down.

"What does Maki say?"

"She understands."

"Well, I don't like it."

Maki worked in a cabaret hostess club in Kichijoji. Apparently she'd quit her job in a karaoke club and started nights at the cabaret around the time Kamiya moved in.

As we got off at Kichijoji, the wind felt colder than in Shibuya, but that might've been because I had got chilled to the core. We passed through the ticket gates and headed out the north exit. The familiarity was soothing. I felt a sense of relief.

"Wanna go to Harmonica Alley?"

"Yeah, let's go."

In a city where even the vomit on the roadside was frozen, people walking the streets knew nothing about us, and we knew nothing about them.

*　　*　　*

The death of the legendary manzai comedian Yumeji Itoshi. I'd watched him and his brother, who were the Itokoi duo, on television ever since I was a kid and they were an inspiration. They showed me that you don't have to be extremely cheerful, or fast-talking, or obnoxiously loud to perform original manzai. When I entered the manzai world, I realized how difficult it is to actually construct a routine using pure narrative technique, without relying on personality to pull it along. Like they did. They were amazing; they brought you back to the basics of manzai and made you understand what it's all about— a supremely funny conversation between two people.

After hearing the news, I couldn't settle. Suddenly I had the urge to practise, so I called up my own manzai partner, Yamashita, and asked him to meet me in the park not far from my place in Koenji. Usually we met at a coffee shop in Shinjuku to think up material, but mostly we came to this park for standing practice. Yamashita wasn't the type to humour me, so I didn't say what prompted the unscheduled call. Unlike me, who liked to rehearse every spare moment, Yamashita didn't like to practise unless there was a live gig coming up.

From the moment I heard the squeak of his bike brakes, I could tell Yamashita was not in a good mood. I suggested we go over material for the next audition, but it did not go well. We seemed to be tuned in to completely different tempos, and although we did our stuff over and over, it only got worse and worse. Yamashita wasn't hearing me. And because he didn't listen, his tone was off. I tried waiting until he finished saying whatever he was saying before coming in, but that meant there was a momentary pause. Which might have been fine in everyday conversation, but not at the manzai speed Yamashita was speaking; it sounded odd, off, like there was a lag. I asked him to listen more carefully.

"What's that gonna do? We've already been over this gag so many times," he replied sharply.

I almost slugged him. The guy didn't understand anything—with attitude like that, we'd never find our rhythm. We could make up new gags every day if we wanted. But that's not what manzai is about. We sat down on a bench and said nothing for a while. The sun was getting low, and the smell of food cooking drifted over from Junjo shopping street behind us. Girls going home from after-school activities walked by our bench, laughing. They were each carrying a long object wrapped in black cloth, a bow or a wooden sword.

"I know practice is important," Yamashita said, "but I have things to do too, you know, so don't call me here without warning."

What the hell was he saying? We both moved to Tokyo to pursue manzai, so nothing was more important. "You should've said that before we came here!" I yelled. I hardly ever raise my voice, but I did then. In the heat of the moment, I leapt up to storm off, but immediately was yanked back down to the bench. The chain on the wallet in my back pocket was attached to my belt loop, and it had got caught in a gap in the bench, so instead of making a grand exit, I found myself back on the bench next to Yamashita. He looked down, suppressing his laughter. Carefully, I pried the chain out with both hands, while he watched the whole process, not saying a word. He made out like nothing had happened while I just looked pathetic.

I went to the toilet to cool off. We'd had many disagreements before, but always over differences in opinion rather than differences in direction. Maybe I was overexcited. Kamiya practised nearly every day with his manzai partner, Obayashi, so I thought it made sense for aspiring young comedians to do that too. When I was done with the lavatory, instead of going back to Yamashita, I rang up Kamiya. I told him briefly about my quarrel with Yamashita, leaving out the wallet-chain fiasco. That might have sounded funny when I didn't want it to.

"I'm ready to hit him," I said.

"If you hit him, you'll break up. Don't raise your fist," Kamiya said gently.

Over the phone I could hear voices in the background, talking and laughing.

"I'm so mad," I said childishly.

I heard Kamiya take a gulp of something and a glass being put on the table.

"When you're finished, come over. We'll eat," he said. "What food do you like most?"

I assumed he was offering me dinner. "Grilled meat," I answered straight.

"No, no. What food do you like most?" Kamiya repeated.

Was he asking me to be realistic about what we could eat at his place?

"What's your favourite food? That's what I'm asking."

Aha, got it. He was doing that Itokoi routine. "It's hotpot."

Kamiya said nothing for a while. A crowd of laughing voices resounded in the silence.

Finally he spoke, "Hotpot, eh?"

"Yes, hotpot."

"You eat pots?"

"No, you know, the stuff that goes with it."

"You must have extremely strong teeth."

"That's not what I mean."

"My teeth aren't strong so I couldn't do it, but what do you like better: metal pots or earthenware pots?"

All of a sudden Kamiya was playing the fool.

"What are you talking about?"

"Which one's easier to chew?"

"No, I don't mean eat the pot."

"Didn't you say you eat hotpot?"

"Yeah, but I meant what's in the hotpot."

"What's in it?"

"Yeah."

"Ah, what's in it! What part of the pot do you peel to get to what's in it?"

"Not like that. I mean hotpot cooked with broth or kimchi, you know, like we always have."

"I get it, you're talking about hotpot cuisine?"

"Yes, of course. Why're you being the idiot all of a sudden? You don't give up, do you. Had me a bit worried."

"OK, then. I'll go buy some cow beef."

"Beef *is* cow, stupid."

Kamiya sniggered at my rudeness. "Oh, that's tough. How about mutton instead?"

"Even tougher."

All the while I could hear this background noise of talking and laughing and now bursts of applause. I bet Kamiya was sitting in front of the television with a drink, shooting the crap with me.

I hung up and went back to Yamashita, regretting having stayed away so long. But I was much calmer now. Yamashita was sitting on the bench with his legs crossed, waving one grubby Jack Purcell sneaker-clad foot in the air and staring at the screen of his mobile phone.

"I'm gonna apologize for three things," he said abruptly.

This was new. He'd never apologized for anything before. Naturally I'd never apologized to him either. That's how it is in a comedy duo, you have this special kind of relationship, kind of hard to explain, but it doesn't include saying sorry for being rude. Not to mention that we'd known each other since junior high and weren't in the habit of saying sorry over each little thing.

"First, I want to apologize for saying I had something more important to do than practise."

It looked like he really was going to apologize for three things.

"Next is for criticizing your material when I never write any myself."

He really was doing this apology thing properly. All of a sudden I felt embarrassed.

"And the last one—" He broke off and went silent.

At first I thought maybe he was too choked with emotion to speak, but it didn't look that way from the expression on his face. He kept spitting on the ground, aiming at the same spot, which was something he always did when he didn't know what to do. Maybe he forgot the third thing he was going to apologize for. He was an idiot in some ways too.

People on their way home brought the bustle of the shopping street with them as they crossed the park. We left it at that and stayed sitting on the bench as if nothing had happened, our words dissolving in the night air.

*　　*　　*

From the window of the train going to Shibuya, I saw cherry trees in full bloom everywhere I looked. So pink-white they were almost blinding. I don't remember when it was I started to hate spring. I turned my attention to the inside of the train packed with students and company employees. The sight irritated me no end.

My life was going nowhere. I spent all day every day practising, but the effort wasn't translating into income. I got by on what I made from working late-night shifts in convenience stores. The nights when I wasn't working I went drinking with Kamiya. It was only the theatre gigs that Yamashita and I did several times a month which made my life worthwhile. I depended on them to get me through the days.

At Shibuya, I made my way through the crowds around the station and walked up Center Street to a building that housed, besides business offices, a small theatre that seated less than a hundred. Theatre D was an important venue for young comedians in Tokyo, where many got their first experience onstage. There used to be a regular live event held here called the Shibuya All-Stars Festival. The agencies would send their up-and-coming comedians along to it, but I never saw anybody who seemed like star material appear here, us included. The only hopefuls to ever enter the cramped dressing room were those young wannabes who had crawled through the streets of Shibuya, dressed in dirty clothing, until they finally got in the door here. I was intrigued by how they all wore different smiles. Some really were smiling with enjoyment. Others smiled uncertainly, not knowing what expression to wear going into the dressing room. Still others had obsequious smiles. And some didn't even notice they were smiling. Not wanting my own face to be observed, I always opened the door quietly and looked down when I entered.

Today the dressing room was a fug of man smell and cigarette smoke. I searched for Sparks on the list of performers and saw we were scheduled third in the first group. Then I saw the Doofuses listed as well, somewhere in the middle. So Kamiya was here today, too.

"Valued customer." I heard the voice and felt a tap on my shoulder simultaneously, and swung around. It was Kamiya.

"Good morning," I said, in the backstage greeting used no matter what time of day or night. "So we're both on today."

Since we worked for different agencies, I almost never ran into Kamiya at shows.

"Yes, we are," he replied with an expression I couldn't read.

We talked, and continued whatever we were talking about as we headed out on to the emergency stairwell where Kamiya smoked a cigarette. He seemed a bit subdued. We chatted right up until it was time for rehearsals to start, and it wasn't until I was on the train going home that evening that the thought occurred to me. A man in a business suit vomited in the railway car I was in, so everyone, including me, got off at the next stop and went into the next carriage. In the mass of people escaping the smell, I was pushed down the centre aisle, pressed tight against other passengers. I twisted my torso so I could breathe better, and did what people do when they find themselves in real tight quarters: look up at the ceiling. And there, hanging in an ad banner, were the words VALUED CUSTOMER. Suddenly it hit me: that was Kamiya's greeting in the theatre. I had made a major blunder! I hadn't processed the innocence of those two words, "valued customer"—they were the perfect opening—and I hadn't responded at all. "*Aaagh*," I groaned aloud, wanting to kick myself.

At the first opportunity I composed a text and zipped it off: *Thanks for today. Just remembered you said Valued Customer when we met in the dressing room. Very sorry I gave a straight answer and blew a unique entrance line opportunity from my sensei. Singing sutras a la Pachelbel*

I got a reply right away: *if u r really sorry please forget. its kindest. thought u didn't hear so decided tomorrow is another day. the messiah of suburbia*

This was tricky. I wanted to know what kind of flow Kamiya had anticipated after that intro, but the moment was lost, it'd be dumb to ask now. Although I sort of knew how Kamiya's mind worked, that didn't mean I knew his actual thoughts. You can't imagine what's in the mind of someone whose talent is greater than your own. Just like it's pointless to look at stab wounds in your flesh and crow over the fact you can tell whose swordsmanship it is. I couldn't give anybody the same kind of stab wounds. I felt like an idiot.

Our ranges of expression were vastly different. Kamiya didn't hesitate to use violent or sexual language for the sake of being funny, while I was afraid of being misunderstood and offending somebody if I did. He didn't have that limitation. He wasn't deliberately trying to be a renegade by talking dirty regardless of who heard it. For him it was purely a process of deciding what was funny and what was not, and not seeing any need to exclude obscenity—if it happened to come up. I had other considerations and tended to weed out the slightest suggestion of anything lewd. If I was trying to paint a picture of a particular scene I had in mind and there happened to be potential for explicit language along the way, I'd turn back from any path leading up to it. Kamiya saw through me and said I wasn't true to myself, that it was a fault. Kamiya kept consistently to his philosophy of using no other benchmark than whether or not something was funny. When I avoided dirty jokes, it was because the part of me that didn't want to be mean or offensive won out over the part that wanted to be funny. That was the part of me that Kamiya said was defective. It's also why Kamiya was the only person I had no objection to using coarse language in front of.

My mobile phone vibrated again: another message from Kamiya. With trepidation I opened it. *tell the truth, we changed our material last minute cos you were there and i wanted to look good. but we didnt win so what was the point. will win next time. crunching tackle by mother teresa*

Reading that brought back more memories of the day, just as I'd been trying to forget it. The Doofuses had taken fourth place and Sparks sixth. These results were decided by audience vote, which meant that already-popular duos and acts who'd invited friends to be in the audience had an advantage, but Kamiya maintained that, apart from family, all votes were up for grabs. Popular duos had once been strangers to their fans and had worked hard to win them over, so it was only fair that they could invite them along. But if a duo didn't perform well one day and their fans voted for someone else, and that duo happened to be eliminated, no matter what their potential, those same fans might be the ones to end their careers. As far as Kamiya was concerned, it took skill to make people think you had potential. Like a guy with no money who convinces his girlfriend he's going to be rich someday, so she's happy to keep supporting him. Still, I thought we should be evaluated based on our performance on the given day. Besides, while Kamiya might have sounded like he was obsessed with winning, he had principles on how go about it to which he appeared to adhere.

Today's winner had been a solo comedian called Shikatani, a rookie in his first year. He had clean-cut features but an unusually long upper lip gave his face an unbalanced appearance, so that all he had to do was to try and look serious and the audience exploded with laughter. His act had been in the form of a lecture on the coolest use of certain words and phrases, which he'd pasted on a flip chart. But he'd overdone it with the glue and the pages kept sticking every time he tried to turn them. Whenever this happened he yelled angrily at the flip chart, "You gotta be kidding, this is bullshit! I was up all night making this!" The audience loved it: his bumbling misfortune coupled with a human vulnerability was a winning combination. He also didn't appear to grasp what was happening, and was half in tears as he vented his frustration at the flip chart, saying over and over, "You gotta be kidding, this is bullshit! People are paying money to see this!" In the end he finished up in a sulk and went offstage.

He's a strange guy. The first time I met him, he came up to shake my hand and said, without even introducing himself, "I like you, Tokunaga. Good meeting ya." Another time he said, casual as anything, "Tokunaga, how about joining the Shikatani Corps as my strategist. Let's rule the country." That's the kind of guy he was. The type I was least comfortable with. After being announced as today's winner, he didn't look pleased in the least; all he did was shout at the audience: "You're joking, this is bullshit! They're all gonna hate me in the dressing room for this." Everybody in the theatre broke down in laughter.

I could've gone on forever obsessing over today's event, but decided to text Kamiya a reply and go to sleep. *The Doofuses were really funny today. From a drainpipe who's the dead spit of your girlfriend.* It wasn't my place to pass judgement on a sempai's act, but it was what I honestly thought. What about Sparks? I suddenly got anxious. The Doofuses had style. Did we? Thinking about this brought on another wave of anxiety. After I got under the covers, another message arrived from Kamiya: *sorry about the time. would a future great come 4th in that place? shouldnt ask a person who was 10th. edison invented darkness*

Here was the thing I was most trying to avoid thinking about. Getting depressed when things don't go well onstage is a gut reaction. It can't be helped. The only way to chase away the blues is to get laughs at the next gig.

On a night like this even Kamiya was jarring. In Tokyo, there are nights when everyone is a stranger.

6th. We came 6th. Edison's invention was a dark basement. I pressed send and forced myself to close my eyes. But all night my chest felt like it was weighed down with lead.

For a stretch I saw Kamiya every day, but there were other periods when we never met. It was during one of those times when a girl I knew from a previous part-time job asked me if I'd be a guinea pig for her to practise dyeing hair. I said yes without really thinking, but there might have been an element of wanting to change myself in it. My long hair was cut short and dyed silver. Then I changed my clothes to all black, to go with the hair. Since I never made any distinction between ordinary clothes and stage clothes, I dressed like this all the time.

I hadn't seen Kamiya for a while. Then one night I received a text from him around ten: *you eat already?* I didn't know what to answer at that hour. Did he really want to eat with me, or did he just want to talk about something? I should've just answered honestly, I suppose, but it was possible Kamiya had already eaten.

I composed a reply: *Sorry, already eaten, but can I join you? The holy pickpocket.* The response was immediate: *hey man, u being polite with me? rice cake*

We met at Kichijoji. Kamiya uttered an uncertain exclamation of surprise when he saw my changed appearance. We walked to Inokashira Park, down the stairs alongside the yakitori restaurant Iseya and through trees shrouded in mist, and when we saw a dazzlingly bright vending machine, our feet naturally made for it. After putting several coins in the slot, Kamiya dug through the purse in his wallet for more. I pulled out a ten-yen coin and stepped up to insert it.

"Leave it!" Kamiya yelled. He continued poking about angrily in his wallet. The coins he'd already inserted came tumbling back out because too much time had passed. Still he kept searching through his wallet.

"That's not going to make any coins appear," I said.

"Think I don't know?! But if you pay ten yen, it's splitting the bill," he said, in a tone that suggested nothing could be worse.

"Kamiya, I just want a bottle of tea. And you only need thirty yen more. I can afford it."

"Are you thick? That's enough!" With a look of resignation he pulled a thousand-yen note from his wallet and put it in the slot to be swallowed up.

We took our drinks to Nanai Bridge and sipped them while we gazed at the lights of large condominium buildings on the other side of the lake.

"Taste good?" Kamiya whispered, peering into my face.

"Yep. If I had a time machine, I'd take this tea back so the grand tea-master Sen no Rikyu could try it."

"Hideyoshi'd probably poke his nose in for a taste too." Kamiya narrowed his eyes in a smile.

"How's your coffee?"

"Delicious. I take back all the times I said 'mighty delicious' at the local noodle shop I went to when I was a kid."

We heard the call of what sounded like a large bird coming from the western side of the park, where there was a zoo.

"Can't that local shop be delicious in your memory too?"

"Nah, nowhere near, compared to this canned coffee. Apologies to the dear old lady."

"That's so sad. They're not even the same thing. They could both be delicious."

The wind lifted the fringe of my hair and ruffled it. Somewhere, a dog barked in concert with the bird.

Kamiya always insisted on paying for me no matter how little money he had or how small or big the cost. That might have been the custom in the entertainment business—the sempai paying for the kohai—but for someone like Kamiya who didn't make much as a comedian, and even worked occasionally as a day labourer, it wasn't easy. We never went to expensive restaurants, but wherever we were he always urged me to order my favourite foods. Which made it all the more shocking when I saw the pile of empty containers of Cup Noodles on the sink in Maki's kitchen. Was that what he was eating at home? When he didn't have money, he borrowed from quick-loan outlets and took me out drinking on that. He called credit cards magic. We went out a lot on money that Maki gave him. He was completely guileless, never pretending, always just saying, "It's Maki's money." I felt terrible when I thought about how hard Maki had to work for the money, but it was also hard seeing Kamiya like that. I didn't understand why it was even necessary for us to go out drinking. I suspected that money—or the lack of it—was behind those periods when he disappeared from sight. So I decided to try and stop him spending so much on me.

Kamiya asked me questions about my silver hair and new look. Black clothes, I said, looked cool with the silver of my hair. He seemed to accept that. Fashion was beyond his ken, but he objected to the idea of fashion trends being expressions of individuality. Even if a look was different or eccentric, that didn't make it solely that person's individual style. It was only the individual style of the person who invented it, and everybody else was just copying. But there were exceptions, for example, like wearing a Pierrot costume all year round. A Pierrot costume might have been created by someone else, but wearing it on a daily basis was original.

"But say that person doesn't want to wear the Pierrot costume in summer because it's too hot but feels they have to, that's when they become an imitation of themselves. Anyone who decides they should look a certain way and lives according to those rules is basically just impersonating themselves, no? That's why I can't get into creating a persona."

This was vintage Kamiya—way out there, pure and exacting, and probably masochistic too. I wouldn't have cared so much, I suppose, if he said all this in his goofy, crazy way, but he sounded like he was on a mission.

"You know what," I began, "I like corduroy trousers, but I won't wear beige corduroy trousers."

"Why?"

"Corduroy trousers have lots of vertical lines in them, right?"

"Yeah."

"Well, beige is the kind of colour that makes you look big, you know, but it clashes with vertical lines that are supposed to make you look slim. People who wear beige corduroy trousers may like to wear corduroy, but they get the bigger picture wrong."

"Man, you are *dee*-tailed. Here I am, thinking we're sort of saying the same thing, but you're on a totally different page," Kamiya laughed.

My thing with beige corduroy trousers had started in

high school. Our Japanese teacher had been mocked for wearing them, but I thought they were cool. I liked the texture, and bought a pair of second-hand navy corduroy trousers that I wore often. So then my classmates made fun of me too. But later when the retro style came into fashion, everybody who'd ridiculed me also started wearing corduroy trousers. I couldn't believe it. Try as I might I could never get over my antipathy for them.

"Enough about beige corduroy trousers. You're just getting off on saying the words."

With this, Kamiya threw his empty coffee can into a rubbish bin. "Drum-drum, drummer boy! Drummer boy in a red cap!" he suddenly burst out singing. "Wake up, dragon! To the beat of the drum!" The eerie melody, if you could call it that, resounded through the night in the park.

We set out walking to Maki's apartment in Kami-Shakujii. I hadn't done this in a long while, and it felt a little like a sentimental journey. In distance, though, it was a long haul, but Kamiya wasn't interested in taking the bus. I have no problem walking around aimlessly for hours, but to trudge long distances as a matter of course like Kamiya did just seemed a little weird.

A bicycle with no lights overtook us, and Kamiya called out, "Don't forget your lights, sir. It's dangerous without them." The rider ignored him. Every time a bicycle without lights went by he repeated this, like a public service announcement. When I said "Forget it", no one was listening, he didn't need to say anything, he just acted like he didn't hear me.

By the time we reached Maki's apartment, I could barely feel my feet. She opened the light-blue door and greeted us with a smile.

"Tokunaga, how are you? Long time no see."

"Yeah," I said, "sure has been a while."

"You'll eat, won't you?"

Maki set about preparing hotpot. I felt a bit uncomfortable showing up like this, even though I'd been a regular guest here at one time. Kamiya was sitting in a different place now, facing me with the television to his right. Maki wore thick kitchen mitts when she brought in the hotpot. I offered to help, but she refused as she always did, and said, "Tokunaga, your job is to eat." There were times when Kamiya and Maki acted like a regular married couple.

We raised our beers in a toast and began the meal. When Maki went to replenish the hotpot, Kamiya got up and announced, "I'm taking a piss." After he'd gone I saw why he had chosen to sit in a different place tonight. Behind his seat was a metal clothes rack with a pair of beige corduroy trousers. Damn, me and my big mouth. I went over and stood outside the toilet, thinking maybe to yell out an apology. I could hear nothing from inside, only the hotpot bubbling again in the kitchen.

"It's ready," Maki said, as she emerged carrying the hotpot back to the table.

When she saw my embarrassed face and where I was standing, she chuckled but said nothing and went back to the kitchen. Her instincts were uncanny.

"Kamiya," I called out.

He too had pretty good instincts. "I got those trousers when I worked at a coffee shop in Osaka," he yelled. "Had to wear a black apron with the name of the shop, and had to wear beige trousers." His voice echoed inside the tiny unit bathroom.

"I'm sorry."

"Don't need your apology. I had to get beige trousers—that's all. I've got several pairs besides the corduroy ones."

I didn't know what to say.

"I needed a few pairs. But corduroy's too hot in summer."

"Yeah, I guess so. But seeing beige corduroy trousers again, I have to say they're cool after all," I said.

"Done," Kamiya said loudly, followed by the sound of water running.

When he came out of the toilet, he put the beige corduroy trousers in a plastic shopping bag and handed them to me. "Here, you have them," he said.

As I was putting them in my backpack and Kamiya was poking at the hotpot, loud, brassy music began blaring from the television. It was the start of a pro-gramme featuring the latest popular young comedy duos. Without a word Maki changed the channel and said brightly, "What would you like to finish up with, rice or noodles?"

"Rice," said Kamiya, his mouth full of tofu. "And throw in any spare body parts you've got in the fridge. We'll finish them up for you."

* * *

Steam rose from the *gyoza* we'd bought at Iseya, mixing with the white breath escaping from our mouths. In the mild winter sunshine, the trees in Inokashira Park looked bleak, as if they needed all the warmth for themselves.

"The season sure makes a difference to the atmos-phere here," Kamiya muttered.

We bought cans of coffee and sat on a park bench looking out at the lake. This place had a good feel about it, as if all the accumulated toxins stored in our bodies could be filtered out just by being here. We both pre-ferred the quiet flow of time in this park to Shinjuku or Shibuya.

A young mother pushing a baby carriage sat on the bench next to us. The baby was wailing loudly, and the mother seemed tired and frustrated.

Kamiya stood up and slowly approached the carriage. "Cute baby," he said to the mother.

She smiled sweetly at the infant, as if reporting Kamiya's words, but it gave no indication of stopping crying.

Kamiya peered at its face. "Two flies settled on a nun's right eye," he said to the baby.

Huh? What was this? Before I could ask, he said in a hammy sing-song voice, "It's some funny haiku about flies I thought up yesterday."

"That's not going to make the baby laugh," I said.

His response was to keep staring at the baby. "Two flies sitting on the grave of a benefactor," he said, smiling.

Evidently he was completely serious about thinking his haiku could be calming, that is. The mother's face began to stiffen in alarm.

"You've got such a healthy baby here," he said to her gently, then continued reciting his fly haiku. The ordinary kindness of his words only seemed to make the fly haiku more bizarre, even scary.

"I am a fly, you are a cricket, that is the sea."

"The flies are the antithesis of Parisiennes."

"A melon from my mother covered in flies."

With each new haiku he recited, he'd cock his head enquiringly at the baby, as if gauging its reaction.

"The baby doesn't think your fly haiku are funny," I said.

He looked mystified. "You try," he said coolly.

I didn't have any experience with babies, but I had a strong feeling that fly haiku were not the right approach. I felt self-conscious in front of Kamiya and the mother—I wished they weren't watching—but I understood that it was silly to be embarrassed in front of a baby.

"Peek-a-boo!" I said in my best baby talk.

The baby kept crying. Kamiya eyed me frostily, but unfazed I tried a few more peek-a-boos.

The mother edged away from me. She stooped down to pick up the baby, and in her arms the baby stopped crying at last. Kamiya did not seem pleased.

"What's with the fly haiku?" I said after the mother had wheeled the carriage away. "A baby's not going to laugh at that."

"Your effort was so not funny," he replied.

"But that's what people always say to babies. Funny doesn't come into it."

"Nope. Definitely not funny."

Maybe Kamiya didn't understand peek-a-boo. How many artists, no matter how pushy, no matter how brilliant, would insist on performing their work unabridged to an audience of one crying baby? Would the geniuses of the world have insisted, as Kamiya did, on entertaining a baby with a full-on performance of their own creation rather than peek-a-boo? I'd been experimenting with getting my ideas across, but Kamiya would never make concessions, whatever the audience. Seemed to me that was putting too much faith in the audience, but when I looked at how resolute Kamiya was in the quest to perfect his style, I felt like a lightweight.

*　　*　　*

Changes at the talent agency. Several comedy duos from another agency got signed with ours, and just like that, Yamashita and I turned into sempai, if only because we were older than some of the new guys. Those kids had it together. In no time they organized a small gig, which was highly successful, showing up Yamashita and me, who'd never organized anything, let alone a gig. All we did was show up at events co-sponsored by other agencies or by some theatre. We wouldn't have known how to pull one off ourselves.

Having these kids on the scene shook things up for me too. Before I knew it, they'd charmed the agency staff. They'd do cheeky things that got them scolded, they'd apologize and the staff would smile like indulgent parents. I'd never seen anything like it. During my few years at the agency, I stepped lightly around the staff, careful not to do anything that'd get me on their wrong side. I never thought I could get them to like me or that I could learn anything from them. The staff seemed to appreciate the way the kids treated them, and really got into dispensing wisdom and all that. Anyway, thanks to these kohai, our comedy division got a shot in the arm. The agency started holding regular live gigs, and Sparks benefited too, of course, but it also meant that we were being compared for the first time.

Up till then we could blame Sparks's lack of success on the agency, or the fact that nobody knew about us. But in a battle between duos in the same agency, we were on a level playing field as far as name recognition went. At the first gig Yamashita and I did our usual routine, which I thought went all right, but the kohai who performed before us didn't hold anything back. They got laughs that could be heard in the dressing room. Even during the fill-in patter at the end, when we were all onstage while votes from the audience were being counted, the new guys let loose and had the audience in stitches. Watching their antics up close, I was totally impressed.

It was also the first time I'd ever felt a complete bonding with an audience. Everything felt distant and unreal; the audience's laughter receded, and things around me blurred. The only thing real was the sound of blood pounding in my ears.

Sparks had been in the business the longest of anyone onstage that night, but we came in sixth out of eight.

Afterwards, the agency threw a party at a teppanyaki restaurant in Shibuya. This was another first, for them to be so generous and so enthusiastic. The restaurant's weekend customers were young people who were coming and going, but better that than the restaurant being empty. I took a seat in the corner, and one of the women on the staff sat down opposite me.

"Tokunaga," she said, "I heard you got drafted for a football team in Osaka. That's great. Why didn't you go on with that?"

This woman always smiled when dealing with us, but I bet she didn't think we were funny at all. She didn't care that I was at the agency. She probably thought I'd be better off playing football for some team in Osaka. And she wasn't the only one. Problem was, when I was in my teens and thinking about my future, if I ever pictured a scene where I *wasn't* doing manzai, I felt sick in my gut. So what was I supposed to do?

NAOKI MATAYOSHI

Yamashita had been at the head of the table, talking with the production writer and stage manager. On his way back from the toilet, he leant over me. "Hey," he whispered, "don't drink in a corner by yourself. Go and talk to the big shots. Manager thinks you should."

I roused myself, beer in hand. It was always like this for me, staying on the fringes and having to force myself to be sociable.

I made my way over to the group standing bunched around the production writer and stage manager, who was a good guy who liked Sparks. The kohai were casually saying just the right thing, putting everyone in a good mood. I was sure my presence would throw a damper on things, but people barely noticed me standing there with a smile pasted on my face. I was alone, not part of the circle. Who was I?

It was Kamiya who zoomed to my rescue. In that moment, when I felt isolated, the odd man out, the thought of times hanging out with Kamiya came to mind. Kamiya always said that everyone is a manzai artist and the only difference is whether they're aware of it or not. Even as I understood how crazy the idea was, somehow the thought of it made me feel better. In Kamiya's company, with his guidance, I'd grown up a lot, but it all crumbled when I tried to fit in. I had nothing to say. I couldn't change my facial expression.

It was the nights I felt I was losing myself that I wanted to see Kamiya most.

*　　　*　　　*

Kamiya was unreachable. Several days in a row I sent him messages saying let's do something—no response. Maybe he was busy. Then I tried ringing, but he didn't pick up. Next day, finally he contacted me and asked me to meet him in Kichijoji. I set out happily, thinking of all the things I wanted to discuss with him. But when Kamiya turned up at two o'clock, his smile was thin and somehow he looked different.

"Not what you thought, eh?" were his first words.

"Huh? What's up?"

"Can you come get my stuff from Maki's place with me?" he said looking down.

"Sure, no problem. But did you two have a fight or something?" I'd often seen Kamiya hassle Maki when he was drunk, but never once did I see Maki get angry with him.

"Maki... she... she got a new boyfriend."

"What? You're joking!"

I couldn't believe it. From what I'd seen, Maki really loved Kamiya. Sure, he gave her a lot of crap, but he depended on her all the same. I always figured they'd get married one day.

"I'm scared, man. You know that Maki works at a kind of cabaret hostess club in Kichijoji, right?"

"Yeah," I said. I had a bad feeling in the pit of my stomach.

"Well, that place is… you know, is for adult entertainment. When Maki first came to Tokyo, she got scouted by someone from this club. So she started working there. Had to dress up like some kind of sexy apparition to serve customers. That's what she did for work… You know her, she can't say no…"

"No, she can't," I said, not knowing what to make of all this.

"But, man, dressing up like a ghost to serve customers—do I need to hear that? I don't want details. You start imagining things." Kamiya looked pained. "I'm a selfish bastard," he mumbled, "but my heart hurts. Really hurts. Maybe I liked her… I probably did."

Seeing Kamiya like this pained *me*. He was probably being vague to avoid getting real emotional in front of me.

"Hey, Tokunaga, how come *you're* crying?" Kamiya laughed.

I didn't know I was crying. But I knew I liked how Kamiya was with Maki.

"It's too early for crying! Save it! We can soak in it over drinks later."

"Don't talk about it like we're going to take a bath."

Oh, this hurt.

"Don't you know anything? You don't jump in without warming up first."

"I said, don't talk like this is a bath."

The pain was painful.

"At least wash your privates before you get in, for crying out loud."

"That makes no sense. What's washing my privates got to do with it?"

The pain was beginning to sting.

"You don't know? Shall I put crying salts in the crying bath for you, for cryin' sake? Make it a teary-coloured bath today?"

"I don't... I don't get it."

Did we have to laugh at a time like this?

"You can't cry before I do. It wrecks my timing."

Kamiya was putting up a valiant front, but you could tell from his voice he was teetering on the edge.

We walked slowly north up Kichijoji Avenue, as if we didn't want to arrive anywhere. A group of smiling primary schoolchildren passed us and stared at me. Was the sight of a grown man crying that weird?

"Hey, the old man with those kids gave me a very

mean eye. Maybe he thinks I'm a mean fuckin' bully, making you cry." Kamiya had to try hard for that one. It wasn't the sort of *hahaha* he usually went for.

"Anyway," he said, barely a few seconds later, "getting back to Maki's new boyfriend, this guy is a customer at the hostess club. A regular. He decides he likes her, and he tells her that. Many times. Then she starts liking him. Apparently."

He said this with a blank expression, deadpan.

Well, Maki *is* beautiful and kind. Lots of men would want to go out with her.

"Kamiya," I started, "all I know is what I see. And I see that Maki really likes you. Maybe she just wanted to get things clear, you know."

"If Maki found someone she likes, I can't complain. She shouldn't waste her life while I try to get my act together. If only I could've done something more for her... I never did. Too late now. What am I going to do, kick up shit? I guess she had no choice."

Kamiya walked slowly, hands deep in his pockets, dragging his feet. We had to stop at almost every traffic light.

"Are you getting all your stuff now?"

"Nah, dunno where I'm going to live, so I can't. I just wanna get a few things and my clothes for the theatre gig tomorrow. The main problem is the new boyfriend's already moved in."

"What?!"

"Maki told him I was just staying there, like a guest. Still, I don't want to go there by myself with him there."

"Yeah, you're right."

Probably the guy wasn't totally clueless. He was probably thinking he was saving Maki from the scum who'd been sponging off her. Getting in there to keep her from going soft on Kamiya. Why else would he move in when someone else still lived there? Probably a part of Maki wanted the same thing.

"If I went by myself and that guy said anything weird, I might kill him. That's why I need you there."

"Because it's easier for the two of us to kill him?"

"Stop! Stop! STOP!"

Kamiya's voice was too loud. Strange, coming from the man who always said that unfunny things should get a low-key response.

As we continued on our way to Kami-Shakujii, he said other things that were so shockingly unfunny it was clear he was unhinged. We passed a house with a nameplate in front, and he said, "Hey, the name is Tokunaga—is this your place?" We heard a siren, and he said, "I thought it was an ambulance, but it's the police." Yeah, hilarious.

"Sorry, Tokunaga."

"What for?"

"I'm scared about this."

"I can go by myself," I said. "And if he says anything weird, then *I*'ll kill him."

I was prepared to do damage to any bastard who'd hurt Kamiya—even if they were in the right. More than anything, though, I wanted to avoid a scene that hurt Maki.

"It's OK, it's OK," Kamiya replied. "I'll do it. Whatever he says, my lips are going to be zipped. But I need you to do me a favour—"

"Whatever you want."

"I don't want to look sad and pathetic, so when we get inside, I need you to get your dick hard and I need you to keep it up the whole time. If I get start to get emotional, I'll just look at your trousers."

"Get my dick hard? What the hell are you talking about?"

"The thought of you getting your dick hard in the service of your sempai during his hour of need will make me laugh, and then I can be cool about it." Kamiya was actually serious about this.

"Isn't that risky for me? What if the guy notices? He'll beat me to a pulp, no questions asked."

"True. But it's such an unusual reason to get beaten up. Think how you can show off the scars on a variety show one day."

"No way. And I know this is not good timing, Kamiya, but I really don't like dirty jokes."

"Didn't hurt when you hung out with me. I'm begging you, man. Just give it a try."

"All right, damn it. I'll do it."

I couldn't believe I was going to do it. I was really going to play the faithful kohai nobly defending his sempai by getting a hard-on. So what did I do? I pulled out my mobile phone to search the Internet for photos of naked women, saving the best for when I was going to need it.

We arrived at Maki's apartment, knocked and stood there nervously, waiting to be let in. Everything looked the same on this side of the grimy blue door, but it was hard even to breathe. Then the door opened.

"Oh, Tokunaga. Thank you for coming," Maki said, greeting us with her usual smile.

Inside the warm apartment my jacket gave off a damp, wintry smell. At the other end of the room—in the spot usually occupied by Kamiya—sat a solid-looking man with a moustache, in workman's clothes. He gave off an air of quiet menace, and didn't bother to look at us as he sat there cross-legged staring at the TV, which had on a rerun of an episode of some drama. Maki would have told him that Kamiya was coming to get his things, but he couldn't have known there would be two of us.

"Excuse us," I said, after clearing my throat.

The man now glanced at us, still without speaking. But in that moment I saw in him a readiness to knife us if necessary. This was a man you could depend on.

Kamiya started throwing his belongings into a bag, making frequent apologies to Maki as he did so. I stood between Kamiya and the man. Maybe I was trying to block Kamiya from the man's sight, or maybe it was the other way round—I don't know. All I know is I felt helpless to do anything else. Maki started to prepare tea for us, but Kamiya stopped her.

"That's everything I need. Sorry to trouble you, but can you throw out the rest, please?" he said to Maki.

I wanted to weep. Kamiya speaking kindly always undid me.

"Sure. I'll tidy up and I can send you anything I think you might want. Let me know where."

Maki's hair looked longer, but that might have been because she was wearing it loose.

How was Kamiya doing? I looked at him. He was looking at my crotch. The guy truly was a fool. Pulling my mobile phone from my pocket, I searched for the grainy photos of naked women I'd saved earlier, and concentrated my best on getting hard. But these were just anonymous nude women who couldn't compete with this drama I was witnessing here, where the complex web of human lives was playing out. Kamiya was still staring at my trousers. That guy's crazy determination... memories of Maki... Kamiya's hopeless kindness... It was up to me to destroy this beautiful world. I don't know where the urge came from but I felt a hardening in my crotch. When Kamiya saw it happening, he burst out laughing.

"We're off then," Kamiya said to Maki, as he slipped on his white All-Star sneakers.

"Sorry to barge in on you," I said, rushing to get out before him.

"Sorry for everything," Kamiya said. "And thanks, eh."

Maki made a face and stuck out her tongue.

Kamiya laughed. "What's that for?" he said and let go of the door.

Smiling, Maki caught the door before it closed. "Take care of yourself," she said. She made one last face, and the door gently clicked shut.

"We're done," Kamiya said.

Back on the street, with wintry wind whipping us, it felt as if we'd been cast out into the world. As we set off, Kamiya clutched his stomach in laughter.

"Oh, man, how can you cry and get a hard-on at the same time? What are you—an oversexed baby?"

"You're the one who told me to."

I would probably never go back to that apartment again. Maybe never go back to Kami-Shakujii either. I wanted to etch this scene in my memory.

"I saw you touching yourself in there. That was cheating!"

"I had to. It was the sayonara of my respected sempai from his kind, generous girlfriend. A naked girl off the Internet wasn't good enough."

Had I been useful to Kamiya?

It was over ten years before I saw Maki again. One day she appeared in Inokashira Park, walking hand in hand with a young boy. Instinctively I hid from her sight. Although a little plumper, she looked much the same as always—truly beautiful, with that stunning smile, the one that made everyone around her happy. I watched as she walked slowly across Nanai Bridge, matching her steps to the boy's. Maybe he was the child of the man in the workman's clothes we saw in her apartment that day—no way I could tell. But just a glimpse of Maki smiling put me in seventh heaven. People can say what they like, but I will never belittle Maki. Maki's life was beautiful. She always smiled at Kamiya and me with her whole heart, dirty and damaged as we were, and in spite of her own wounds. Nobody can ever take that beauty away from Maki. The boy who held her hand will be the happiest boy in the world. He'll always see her face up closer than anyone else. I envy him.

Rays of early summer sun were reflecting off the surface of Nanai Pond, scattering into beads of light. Kamiya would say I should've jumped into the pond to make Maki laugh. But I didn't want to do anything that could destroy this lovely scene. Whatever anyone says: Maki's life was beautiful. That boy will be the happiest person in the world.

*   *   *

After Kamiya left Maki's, he couch-surfed at various acquaintances' for the next six months. I went with him everywhere, looking for a place to live, but even in far and inconvenient locations, it was difficult to find anything halfway OK. Finally, he found an apartment in Mishuku, between Ikejiri-Ohashi and Sangenjaya, which was cheap and not too far from Shibuya.

I felt pain from the loss of Maki too, and neither of us was our self at that time. We did things like buying matching table-tennis outfits and playing all night at a table-tennis joint in Shibuya. Or going drinking, when Kamiya would pay the bill of some guy we hadn't even talked to, then watch his bewildered expression as we left. Or going to karaoke places and belting out heart-felt macho songs by Tsuyoshi Nagabuchi and Takuro Yoshida. Or getting bento lunches and picnicking in the Showa Memorial Park in Tachikawa. Kamiya got into the habit of dropping his trousers and mooning me in public, somersaulting and singing, "Young man, young man, young man—your gateway to success!"

His debts ballooned. But seeing how Kamiya lived while I kept working late-night shifts at a convenience store in Koenji made me feel small and disgusted with myself. I was earning the minimum necessary to live in Tokyo, but even with the little I made as a comedian on top of that, I was a long way off the average income for my age. Sometimes I thought Kamiya was on the nobler path, being an artist 24/7. But that took a lot of guts and determination.

We were on our way to the Futako-Tamagawa river flats with some cheap prepared food from the Marusho store in Ikejiri-Ohashi for our dinner. We had walked for nearly two hours, me holding on to a can of coffee all the way.

"Attaboy," Kamiya said, "carry around canned coffee like that every day and your right hand will morph into a coffee holder."

"Yeah, that'd be handy, but I'd only be able to write with a pen the size of a can," I replied.

The food was in my backpack, and I worried the fried chicken was making my bag stink, so I suggested we find somewhere close to stop and eat. Kamiya rejected the idea outright.

"Fried chicken is supposed to get you drooling, but the second you smell it in your backpack, you think it stinks. You're choosing to delude yourself."

I was not convinced.

"Much ado-doo, much ado-doo," he said annoyingly.

What could I say to that? That childish retort had such perfect pitch that any response was futile. Kamiya probably invented the nonsensical phrase—on the spot!

Whenever I was with Kamiya, all the brain cells I never used in ordinary daily life got a workout, which was exhausting, but Kamiya was so wild and unpredictable that I could forget life's hassles for a while. Even if he didn't know any limits, I could talk with Kamiya. I couldn't with other people. A part of me must have been convinced he had all the answers.

"You don't you care what people think, do you, Kamiya?" I asked, as we trudged along, now passing Komazawa-Daigaku Station. The question wasn't entirely out of the blue. It was something we'd talked about before, but now that Sparks was starting to get theatre gigs, I was hearing more stuff about our act and thinking about it more.

"I don't like it when people sound off, but I don't really care."

"Yeah, but what about the Internet? Don't you care when you get trashed there?"

"Ah, those motherfuckers. Do I look cool about it to you?"

"Yes."

"Well, there's a lotta lies out there. But I check them out when I don't have anything better to do."

I was nervous continuing this line of talk. I'd been trolled lately—something other comedians told me was par for the course—and I wanted Kamiya to blow it all off for me, make me feel better. But he wasn't doing that, seemed to be holding back. Could I take what he had to say?

"Some people say you shouldn't fight back because it puts you on the same level as the fuckers who write all that shit," he began. "What's that supposed to mean?"

I was probably one of those people.

"What the hell does 'level' mean anyway?" he went on. "We're all supposed to be human, right? If someone makes a mistake, just tell 'em. I learnt in kindergarten you shouldn't do things other people don't like. Fact is, kindergarten taught me a lot. Not everything, maybe.

But how to say thank you, and sorry. And be grateful for your food. Decent shit. The people that diss me are kind of like kindergarten dropouts."

I was on his side there.

"Those trolls who trash people on the Internet. Well, if they say something legitimate—about, like, your artistry or delivery—it can't be helped. It's OK, it's the way it is. But if you let it get to you, not good. When people throw their knives, it can draw blood—I'd rather be punched. Whatever, you're supposed to put up with it. Even though you're bleeding. Even if you might wanna kill yourself."

"Yeah, I don't know how to handle it."

"But this is how I see it. If trolling's the only thing the troll's got going for him, if he needs it to get through the night, well, OK, bring it on, I say. Go ahead, slag my character and treat me like I'm subhuman. I won't like it, but I'll survive. Say the shittiest, most hurtful thing you can think of—great! I'll be fucking furious. But I really believe when you get trolled, you gotta get that anger out of your system. Don't just let it all roll off you—take that malicious bullshit head-on and call it out for what it is: malicious bullshit. Don't be hypocritical and say you get where the troll's coming from, don't offer cheap sympathy and pretend they got a point, so they'll forgive you not being the way they want you to be. But it's frigging exhausting to argue. Some people love to argue, but it only wears you out.

"Say you're a troll, you hurt someone, the satisfaction only lasts a moment. One brief moment. And while you're feeling satisfied, nothing changes. For sure, nothing changes for the better. You put people down only to make yourself feel better, or important, or whatever. But in the meantime you don't mature. You're stuck as a troll. That's pitiful. You're a victim. Committing slow suicide, in my opinion. Trolls are in the same category as drug addicts. No way you should do drugs, but if a person's an addict, someone has to help them quit. So you have to tell them: trolling's the easy way out, but you're wasting your time. Give it up while you still have a life."

Well and good, even brilliant, but there was nothing to be gained for me in standing up like that.

"Does what they say bother you?" Kamiya asked.

"The responses on the questionnaires get to me a lot."

"Ah, those surveys they hand out to audiences at the theatres. What about the Net?"

"Yeah, that too."

I got into manzai because I wanted to do comedy, so when I hear I'm not funny, it cuts pretty close to the heart.

"If you care too much about what people say, you'll only get tired. Does it make you change what you do?"

"Nah."

"See. We're not that slick. Do what you want. If you're good, you can eat; if you're not, you get dumped. That's all it is, right?"

That's all it was supposed to be. Is that all it was for Kamiya? For me, I wasn't sure.

By the time we arrived at the river flats, the reddening in the western sky had reached the clouds above our heads. We sat side by side, eating potato salad and cold, tough fried chicken. I brought my backpack up to Kamiya's face with the zipper slightly open and he thrust his nose in.

"Whoah," he exclaimed, backing away.

Though Kamiya revelled in his bad boy image to a certain degree, he was friendly in the extreme to people he liked. Especially towards anyone who once got close to him. That didn't mean I was any less wary of him, though. No matter how kind he was, his ideas about humour often left me feeling small.

We were walking in Setagaya Park. All around us the leaves were turning the colours of autumn, all but one tree, a maple, which remained stubbornly green.

"Master, why is this tree the only tree with green leaves?"

"Because the new guy forgot to paint it," Kamiya promptly replied.

"Does God have a department for that?" I asked.

"No. It's the guy in work clothes. The one with a holey sock and a missing front tooth," Kamiya said, with an undertone of sudden irritation.

I just let it hang there.

"You know, Tokunaga," he said, "if I say something that makes no sense, you always try to make it make sense by filling in the gaps. That's a talent too, but you're nuts if you have to make everything neat. I say something strange but you can't let it be—it's all gotta be real, right? The person who paints the leaves is a man with a hole in one sock and missing a front tooth. His daughter wants to go to an expensive private school with a big brass band, so he's working his butt off to make the tuition, but the daughter can't stand the smell of his sweat or his hair in the bathtub. Right?"

"Yes, that's right." How else could I answer?

"So if a rookie god forgot to paint the maple or a dirty worker forgot to paint the maple, whose fault is it? Who's more likely to be real?"

"The man, of course."

"Fucking right!"

"Why're you so mad all of a sudden?"

Kamiya proceeded to put on a show of being angry now, making out like he hadn't been from the start, but I think what really upset Kamiya was that his gag had got twisted halfway through and he was frustrated. Moments like this were a real bummer. Kamiya could tell on a gut level if something was funny—as opposed to wild or outrageous, or a question of technique that allowed the audience to get it. My gut was nowhere near so advanced. I could never get to his level.

I could smell fresh earth rising from the roots of the maples. The trees swaying in the wind cast their shadows on our path. I stroked my face with both hands, as it threatened to twitch.

My mobile phone rang, from a number I didn't recognize. I didn't pick up, but listened to the recorded message: "Obayashi here. Call me when you get this."

Obayashi was Kamiya's partner. What did he want? The unwritten rule of manzai was that members of a duo kept away from younger comedians their partner was friendly with. It wasn't a hard-and-fast rule or anything, just an understanding to keep things simple.

Obayashi and I met near Koenji Station and went to a nearby *yakitori* shop. Inside, a variety entertainment programme blared from the old television, the screen darkened by smoke from the grill and grease.

"You doing all right?" Obayashi asked.

He downed his beer in one gulp and immediately ordered another. Kamiya had told me about this habit.

"He thinks he's Popeye or something," Kamiya had said. I didn't know if Popeye drank beer.

"Yeah, same old same old," I said. "But hey, you're not wearing your wooden clogs today."

"Never worn clogs in my life!"

Fact is, Obayashi always wore heavy work boots.

"Did you leave the dog tied up to a utility pole?"

"You're thinking of someone else!"

Obayashi's voice, unlike Kamiya's, was naturally loud.

"Is it OK for you to be out in public?"

"Hey, who'd recognize me!"

I had this thing with Obayashi that whenever we met, I always spoke to him as if he was Saigo Takamori, the last samurai. We'd been doing this shit for over five years, even if Obayashi still hadn't figured out he was Saigo Takamori. I liked him a lot, but we kept our distance. He could be insensitive sometimes.

After he finished his second beer, Obayashi got to the point. "Listen, in case you don't know, Kamiya's up to his neck in debt." He looked pained, and he made no effort to lower his voice.

"Yeah, I know."

Kamiya was lousy with his money. He spent without thinking, and often when we went out, he had to get a quick loan first. Ever since breaking up with Maki,

Kamiya had been floundering. It was masochistic the way he didn't seem at ease unless he was suffering.

"He tries to look cool in front of you," Obayashi went on, "but he doesn't know when to stop, and if he keeps getting deeper and deeper in debt, we might not be able to do manzai any more."

Probably Obayashi didn't want to be saying this kind of thing to a kohai, but maybe he thought he had no choice.

"It's my fault," I said quickly. "He insists he's supposed to pay for me."

Obayashi clamped his lips tightly together. "Nah, it's not your fault. Kamiya, when he talks about you, is always pumped."

He was a good guy, Obayashi, and Kamiya was lucky to have a partner like him. He was ambitious, though. When he said, "I wanna be big," I pretended not to hear.

"Hey, it's Shikatani." Obayashi had turned to look at the television.

I turned to look too.

Shikatani had been discovered by a big-name programme host. The guy put him on his show and treated him like his favourite toy. And Shikatani was making the most of it, happy to be the darling of the moment. He had the knack of letting his emotions loose in a way that everyone made fun of. But that's what everybody needed. He made them feel better. On entertainment programmes he laughed harder than anyone, cried more than anyone and was so restless he couldn't sit still. Once on candid camera he was served sushi that had gobs of nasal-burning wasabi in it. He went crazy, shouting, "You shouldn't ruin good food with too much wasabi!" Another time he fell for a woman who it turned out the programme had set up for him, but he wasn't embarrassed about it in the least. "Don't underestimate the power of love," he said. He was loved by all and forgiven anything. Nobody could beat him at what he did. He had a pure kind of magnetism that you couldn't pull your eyes away from.

Obayashi watched his antics with admiration. "That Shikatani was born with more manzai gags than we could dream of in ten years," he said.

I hated that he was right. It made me want to scream. Instead, I gritted my teeth and said nothing, wishing I could grind my teeth into powder.

*　　*　　*

Kamiya's thirty-second birthday. That night, I texted him birthday greetings. Almost at once I got a reply:

there was four years between us when we met. funny how its still the same

Then another text: *you seem busy these days. still writing my biography?*

Of course. I had a stack of a dozen notebooks filled by now. In the beginning I wrote about Kamiya and Kamiya only, but then I started jotting down ideas for gags and odd thoughts, so now it was more like my own diary.

Another text (which meant Kamiya must be alone): *i suppose its not funny*

Make it funny, please I replied.

dunno if i can

You could run for governor of Tokyo

nobody would laugh at that

Since when had Kamiya turned into such a wimp? Was he drinking cheap booze alone? I should've invited him out earlier but thought he'd be out with the kohai from his agency. And I didn't want him having to look out for me in case I couldn't hold up in front of them.

Sparks was beginning to get more attention after we started appearing on a late-night TV programme popular with young people. Magazines were mentioning our name, and it was getting to the point where a few people even recognized me on the street and called out to me.

I was twenty-eight. If anyone was a diehard comedy fan, they might have heard of me now. But whenever somebody like the young hairdresser I went to asked what kind of work I did and I answered comedian, they said, "Wow, my friend's going to comedy school." I didn't know what to say. I'd just sit there with a vague smile on my face, and stare at myself in the mirror.

At the agency, new kohai kept arriving. At first they had been rather cliquish, but with each live show the agency put on, the barriers broke down, and now I was on easy terms with them. The more I talked to them, the more I realized how unique Kamiya was: he had high ideals and set himself to do big things. And there was no doubt about his talent and appeal. My time with him had been about learning the comedy world. But I also began to see how he might have been using me as a canvas for his theories about comedy—and how I was starting to suffocate.

According to Obayashi, Kamiya tried to act cool in front of me. Partly that was just the way he was, but I was probably an accomplice in helping his vision of comedy balloon to the point where it became difficult for him to live it. His attitude, and his declarations that he didn't give a damn what people thought, made it look like he believed he wasn't losing even when he was. People were scared of him. And things that scare people have to be eliminated, so the fools and the weird get scorned. That's how society works. Kamiya became the target of ridicule. He was called a fool, and laughed at for not following success.

The big event at Zepp Tokyo, where young comedians gathered for the chance to show their stuff to the movers and shakers in the TV and theatre world. Each manzai duo got to perform two sets.

The Doofuses drew loud laughter with their first act. But then for their second act they repeated exactly the same dialogue, except this time it was played over loudspeakers with Kamiya and Obayashi lip-synching along. After a while their lip movements became unsynchronized, eliciting uneasy laughter from the audience. Then halfway through Obayashi punched Kamiya in the head, and Kamiya held his head in both hands and stopped performing. But their witty dialogue continued pouring from the speakers, and now their actions were completely disconnected from their words. This got the most explosive laughter of the day from the audience. The judges, however, were not amused: "We watched one duo who used sound equipment. We would like to stress that this is not manzai."

Other comedians, though acknowledging the audience reaction, piled on, saying the routine was not funny.

It was the safe thing to do: to dismiss the Doofuses as weird—a joke at manzai's expense. Of course they were conveniently ignoring the first straight routine. They now had licence to put Kamiya down. "Don't you wanna be a success?" they laughed derisively. Kamiya didn't say anything, just looked displeased.

None of it would've been a problem if the Doofuses had performed this as an action sketch at a gig put on by their agency. But to Kamiya, causing a disturbance in front of an audience who'd come to see manzai was in itself funny. That interested me—what could come next. How he could proceed to demolish something they had just done successfully, the orthodox way. Whether it really is manzai or not wasn't important. This was pushing the boundaries, but nobody would give Kamiya a place to do it.

Anyone who doesn't pander is bound to make enemies, and Kamiya had his own theories and beliefs. No matter where he was, or whether the audience wanted to hear it or not, he always said what he wanted. Some comedians applauded this stance but others avoided him because of it. Me, I just wanted to be like him. Still, I was who I was—I could never be like him.

Kamiya had other kohai under him at his agency too. Increasingly, they and the kohai from my agency came along when we hung out. I was a bit sad about this, missing his exclusive attention, but it was inevitable. I became friendly with the kohai from my agency who attached themselves to me, and when they expressed scepticism about Kamiya, I didn't hesitate to doubt their talent.

* * *

Early one evening, I asked Kamiya if he wanted to go out for something to eat. He had a date lined up later, he said, but was happy to have a couple of drinks before that. We were to meet at seven o'clock outside Ikejiri-Ohashi Station, and when I got there, the leaves on the ginko trees were in their full autumnal glory. It was awesome, though I was disappointed at how prosaic my reaction was.

Then Kamiya appeared, and I could hardly believe my eyes. His hair was a beautiful silver, and he wore a tight-fitting black shirt with skinny black jeans and black desert boots: in other words, he was dressed in my style! He could not have been unaware of what he was doing. I'd been dressing like that for several years now—going to some trouble over it—onstage and off.

"Kamiya, what's with the outfit?"

"I didn't know you had to bleach your hair before putting in the silver dye. My head sure hurt," he said, running his fingers through his hair.

He was dead serious—this wasn't a joke of his, though it should have been.

We went to our usual place, an old pub near the station. Its speciality dishes were Japanese—deep-fried pork cutlet with miso and *hegi* soba noodles—but for some reason, when you entered the pub, you were greeted with a line-up of old Western-style dolls. Since Kamiya was to have dinner at some girl's apartment later, we only ordered some pickles to nibble on while sipping our shochu-and-water. Time went by as we caught up, the clock showed it was already past midnight, but Kamiya gave no sign of leaving. "Shouldn't you go soon?" I asked.

"Nah, I'm feeling good. Haven't been out with you in a long time." Kamiya's judgement always slipped grossly when he was drunk.

I was happy to be there with him, but although I felt bad for the other person, I couldn't very well force him to leave. I was drinking at the same pace as Kamiya and was now also very drunk too, but more than anything, I was hungry. Like starving. We'd been drinking while eating nothing but pickles for the last five hours. I could have ordered something, but then Kamiya'd end up fighting me to pay for it and I didn't want him to do that.

"I gotta piss," Kamiya said, standing up. "Let's have one more glass, then go."

Now was my chance. If I ordered something small, maybe he wouldn't notice. Immediately I called the waiter over and ordered a sausage selection.

Kamiya was slow in coming back—maybe he was vomiting in the toilet—so I had time. But when the waiter returned with my order, he brought a sizable tabletop charcoal burner on which I was supposed to grill the sausages. Which was the exact moment Kamiya got back to the table.

"Wow, you ordered this?"

I could've sunk through the floor. I was starving, but now I was embarrassed.

"I'm really sorry. I didn't know it'd be like this."

"If you're that hungry, let's eat up, and then you're coming with me," Kamiya said.

And so it was decided that I would be a guest for dinner at the girl's apartment.

Next thing I knew, after two more drinks while we finished the sausage, it was three in the morning. We walked along the highway through Sangenjaya, entered Setagaya Avenue, then walked some more until residential areas appeared on our right. The girl's apartment was on a corner. Kamiya climbed the stairs—he'd obviously been here before—and rang the doorbell. The girl, who

I was meeting for the first time and who had been waiting so long, opened the door as if it was a normal hour.

I apologized for barging in in the middle of the night.

She looked at me. "Oh, wow, it's Tokunaga," she said
smiling.

Her name was Yuki.

"Toldya he's a buddy," Kamiya boasted.

The low table was set, laid out with a large plate of
vegetables and a small hotpot over a gas burner. The
cooking chopsticks and ladle stand were just like you'd
see in a restaurant, and the sight of them filled me with
embarrassment. Yuki, however, showed no sign of dis-
pleasure as she went efficiently back and forth to the
kitchen, getting things ready.

Yuki was fat. There was no other way to put it. The
word chubby did not come remotely close to describing
her. But her skin, under the fluorescence of the light, was
beautiful, almost translucent, and gave off a feeling of
total cleanliness. And, like someone else we knew, she
laughed often. The sound of her laughter bouncing off
the white walls began to merge in my mind with Maki's
voice.

What a long way I'd come without realizing it.

Racked by shadowy guilt and fear and with an uncertain future, somehow I'd clawed my way this far. I'd
been fired from my late-night job after taking time off

without notice to appear in an all-night programme, a gig that had come up suddenly. A kid younger than me at my next part-time job gave me a weird nickname. But lately, finally, I'd been making a living solely from performing manzai. If I could make a little bit more, I might be able to send money back home to my family. Maybe I could invite them to come see me in a theatre once, and afterwards we could go out for a nice meal.

The trademark music of the manzai programme blared from the TV. "Sparks is on soon!" Yuki announced excitedly.

She laughed indiscriminately at all the preceding acts, while Kamiya simply stared at the screen. Then it was time for Sparks. The intro music started up, and there I was, standing with Yamashita in front of the microphone. Yuki laughed even more now. Kamiya didn't move, didn't say anything. His face had turned pale. Laugh, I pleaded in my heart. But Kamiya didn't laugh. The irritation churning in my chest dropped into my gut. I'll slug him, said a voice in my head, this is making me mad. Why's he wearing the same clothes as me? The routine finished.

Yuki had laughed the whole way through. She was laughing even after our act was done. But Kamiya wasn't laughing.

"No good?" I asked, my voice quavering.

"Yeah, you could say that," Kamiya said, looking down as he skimmed the scum off the surface of the simmering broth. "Why don't you do more of the funny stuff you like doing?"

It was a sincere response. Then the ladle slipped from his hand and ended up upside down in the hotpot, looking just like a microphone in the soup.

"I can't," I said. Blood rushed to my head. I *can't*. If Kamiya was going to tell me my manzai wasn't funny, well, there was nothing more I could do.

I was different from him. I wasn't a total nonconformist, but on the other hand, I wasn't so smooth that I fit right in. I wasn't proud of that either. Because it wasn't honourable for a man to tell lies. And yes, I do know how banal that sounds. Still, although I might have felt bad, it was impossible to do the kind of stuff he wanted me to do. Recently I'd learned to put ego aside. I'd learned the trick of pleasing an audience, and could do it without compromising, pretending or lying to myself. If Kamiya would just pat me on the back for that, I'd be a happy man. *As if.* I was getting the laughs, so I thought maybe Kamiya would laugh, too. But no, he never cracked. I could make him laugh offstage, hopeless fool that I was, but when I got onstage, I might as well have been...

What *did* he think was funny anyway? What did I have to do to make him laugh? If he said it was funny to spoil a beautiful scene, I went and spoilt a beautiful scene. He was right. As a performer, it was the right thing to do.

But maybe I'd been lying to myself.

Kamiya was a genuine fool. He repeated his fool's mantra in that musical voice of his, and he scraped a living on what little he made. I desperately wanted to be like him, I wanted to throw off everything unnecessary and live like that, too.

I also wanted to be funny, but interesting too. The sort of person who could pull it off in any situation at any given moment: that was Kamiya—the embodiment of funny. He was always funny when we were together, and when we were onstage together, he at least tried. I was faithful to what he taught me and I wanted to be like him—the kind of entertainer who pursues their art head-on and makes no excuses. I wanted to be funny in the purest sense, with no impurities.

Kamiya's idea of funny was the words he hadn't yet spoken. The creative thought that hadn't been expressed. In other words, anything that reached beyond his own talent. He challenged himself all the time, he pushed his limits and he was always in the moment, enjoying it, which is why he was irrepressible. You couldn't hold the guy back. He created something, then wrecked it, as if he couldn't give a shit. It was totally refreshing. There was nothing like it.

Not everybody liked it. They said Kamiya was avoiding responsibility, but they were missing the point. Kamiya never backed away from what he believed was genuinely amusing. He always gave 100 per cent trying to make people laugh his way, even if his audience was a red-faced baby. Maybe he was misunderstood, but he wasn't running away from anything.

He wasn't playing to the public, he was after something you couldn't touch, something that someday might make society pay attention. He lived a pure kind of life, solitary, lonely maybe, but maybe loneliness was the inspiration for him. That wasn't for me, though. In the end I couldn't ignore public opinion. That was where the real hell was, but Kamiya didn't understand that. As long as society was reflected in my eyes, he couldn't escape it though. He fought public opinion without compromising his ideals.

For someone like me, who could only be conventional, the only option was to put everything into following that path. It was noble of Kamiya to flatly reject it; that was his business, but I couldn't help hating him for it, damn him...

He had this thing about the reason a path existed was so we didn't have to follow it. Finally, it was dawning on me that the path he was on, way ahead of me, was the path I needed to get off.

"That's not what I meant."

His voice was like a reality jolt. The manzai programme was over, and an infotainment programme was now on. Yuki, maybe sensing the tension, had left the table.

"It wasn't that funny, I guess," I said. But despite saying this, I knew that I had to take a stand against him.

"I didn't say it wasn't funny," he said. "But I know you, Tokunaga. You are funny and you can do better." He spoke softly, as if the words were difficult to say.

"So why don't you go on TV and try."

He made a dismissive sound through pursed lips.

"Why don't you go audition and be funny on TV instead of just complaining about me not being funny enough?"

"Yeah, right." Kamiya did not look at me.

"I'm just like you. And it's not just me—all entertainers like us have routines we think are funny. But what's the good if people don't hear them? If you don't make the effort to be popular, and nobody hears, it'll be like the genuine funny stuff never existed."

"You think too much. Loosen up and just do what you like."

"That's OK if manzai's just a hobby. But if you love it and want to keep on doing it, you gotta make the effort."

Kamiya said nothing. Maybe he was thinking.

"You can't throw everything away. I set my filter fine because I absolutely don't want to get rid of anything. It means a lot of crap gets in too, but even I can chuck that stuff anytime. So please, don't be proud only of being able to throw stuff away."

"Tokunaga, I'm sorry," Kamiya said softly.

I wish he'd slugged me instead.

"And another thing—why the hell did you copy my hairstyle? And my clothes. You said you'd rather die than copy somebody, that you wouldn't even want to imitate yourself... Well, look at you, are you copying me or what?"

I really didn't want to be saying these things, but I couldn't help it. I also didn't have to hear Kamiya's response to know what he was feeling.

"I just thought your hairstyle looked cool."

Was that all it was? All that mattered to him was his art—his unique ideas about comedy and expression— and he had zero interest in hairstyle and clothes? Was copying my style no different from his ordering the same thing at a restaurant that somebody else ordered because it looked good? Did he eat the same thing as everyone else while he was thinking up gags only he could come up with? Style for me was something personal, like the frame you put on a picture. It was the way you displayed yourself, the way people might see you, have an impression of you. But you did it so they would buy the picture. Maybe that was of no concern to Kamiya, the artist. But it was for me, because I believed that the frame was part of the picture, and if you completely ignored commercial considerations, you ran the risk of changing its original meaning. It was like not protecting your work.

"It's copying," I said shakily.

A heavy silence descended between us. I sat still, unable to move. Kamiya stood and, with an air of sadness, went over to the chest of drawers and rooted around in it. He pulled something out and went swiftly into the bathroom.

What had I done? Was I trying to make Kamiya take responsibility for my lack of ability? No! I'd spoken my honest truth, exposing all the ugly, embarrassing parts of me in the process because I hoped Kamiya would turn it around for me.

He emerged from the bathroom looking like a different person. His hair had been cut every which way, jagged, like a crazy man, shorn to the scalp here, long strands there. It was so hideous it was shocking. I could hardly bear to look at him.

"I was trying for a Beckham look but ended up more like a cheetah."

"You wish!" I said, and Kamiya laughed.

"Hey, sorry about all that," he said, and went over to the fridge for a bottle of saké.

I don't remember how I got home that night. The next day I phoned Kamiya, but he wasn't answering. I texted an apology, and immediately the reply came back: *No problem. I was drunk and don't remember a thing!* It was the exclamation mark that left me feeling strangely sad.

The manzai TV show we were on folded after a year. Doing the show had brought us a lot, though. Like invitations to appear on late-night shows, open-mic comedy nights and campus events all around the country, not just in Tokyo. I'm sure that the other comedians who got these gigs knew like we did that our fans were young and fickle, and our popularity would never last. We were too old to make the mistake of thinking otherwise. And we were almost too old to think it was our job to pretend we didn't know—and to be sneered at because of that. But I lived for that moment— always incredible to me—when you run towards the mic in the centre of the stage and cheers rise up from the crowd.

I moved from a shabby apartment with no bath that was 25,000 yen a month, to a classier place in upmarket Shimokitazawa that was 110,000 yen a month. It might've looked like I was getting in above myself, but I knew what I was doing. Just once in my life I wanted the experience of living in a place like that.

Yamashita got a girlfriend and was living with her in trendy Ebisu. He even started talking about getting married.

Kamiya, I hadn't seen since that night at Yuki's.

In the end the Doofuses never got asked to be on the shows in which the other comedians in our generation appeared. You could tell who got on them and who didn't from their lifestyles. But lavish lifestyles, like fame and trendiness, don't go on forever. I knew this truth, of course, even as I hoped against hope I could hold on. Eventually, some of the manzai duos in those shows made their way on to prime-time TV, while others disbanded. They might make fresh starts as solo comedians, or switch direction to become producers and scriptwriters, or go back to their home towns and find different jobs entirely. Much of my time as a comedian had been spent with Kamiya, but in recent years it was the kohai from the agency I saw most.

I'm not a sociable person, and didn't get to know many other comedians. Nevertheless I thought of them as my peers, comrades battling in the same theatres at the same time as me, and I was proud to be associated with them. Whenever I entered a dressing room in my dirty Converse sneakers, they'd be there, dressed just as scruffily as me. Being with them let me forget for a moment about getting left behind in life and being made fun of as just-another-comedian. It was a way of fending off reality. We may not have ever exchanged a single word, but if it hadn't been for them, I could never have stuck with that crazy life for ten years.

And then slowly, I began to realize that things were changing. Yamashita and I were getting fewer and fewer gigs, and the kohai began leaving to head down new paths. I can say for a fact, though, that we were never just fooling around. We put it all on the line. We knew fear, lodged like a stone in the pits of our stomachs. Fear of all the things there were to fear: parents ageing, lovers getting old and not succeeding before time ran out. I dreaded having to put an end to my dream.

There were many nights when everybody was a stranger. But we kept on doing our thing and refining our gags, with genuine feeling and hope, and drinking with the little money left over at the end of the month to ease the anxiety and forget about the hardship. I'd find myself getting pumped up thinking things could still change and we'd change the world. Everybody believed, absolutely, that their day would come.

One afternoon Yamashita rang up to say let's meet. Without asking why, I set out for the coffee shop where we always went. When I saw him sitting at our usual table, I knew from the look on his face this was going to be heavy. He told me he'd married his girlfriend, and she was pregnant with twins. Our manzai partnership was over.

"I know it sounds lame when I say I'm doing this for my unborn children," Yamashita said, "but it is true they've given me a push." He looked relieved.

Yamashita wasn't suddenly throwing it all away, I thought. He was moving on to a new challenge.

"Congratulations," I said.

Then: "You know, I should really get busy and find a place where the three of us can live with the twins."

He didn't miss a beat. "Yeah, how cool if we could all live together!"

I was a bit embarrassed at the way our roles in the duo were so clearly on display, but Yamashita kept it going neatly.

"How would we explain it to her parents?" he said, still pushing me into being the funny man, as always.

This coffee shop with its dirty walls was not a place we frequented because it was popular with a certain crowd. We came because it was comfortable, because we could always find a couple of seats and because we never got the slightest inkling we weren't welcome. When I thought about never coming here with Yamashita again, I felt a sentimentality even for the coffee cups.

I wanted to say thanks for the last ten years, but knew my voice would shake, and maybe he wouldn't hear me properly, and maybe I'd have to repeat myself. So I left the words unsaid.

We told the agency Sparks was disbanding. Nobody tried to stop us. The break-up would become official once we completed any remaining engagements on the books.

Word got out. At our last gig for the agency, the audience was bigger than usual. Apparently we'd connected with some people. We were manzai artists in some eyes at least.

The music starts, I emerge from the wings, turn to the mic and take a bow. Yamashita bursts out from behind, overtakes me, and I follow him into the blaze of lights. Loud applause as we run towards the mic. How many times have we worn these matching tight black suits, chosen when we were twenty, on the occasion of our coming-of-age ceremonies, specifically for our future manzai career. We'd never learned to wear decent shoes until we became adults. Now we stand with the mic between us.

Yamashita touches it lightly. "Thank you," he says, "we're Sparks."

Applause rolls through the small theatre.

"I chose to do manzai," I begin, "because I wanted to turn common sense on its head. But all we've turned on its head is that fine saying about effort being rewarded."

"What a bummer!" Yamashita breaks in energetically. The laughs rise up.

"This is what I'm thinking: do you ever get so carried away with emotion you can't say what you want properly?"

"Ah, maybe."

"So this is my idea. I say everything opposite to what I really mean. That way I can be sure I get my feelings across."

"You certainly make everything complicated right to the very end, don't you?"

"Just give it a try. Ready?"

"OK."

"Hey, partner!"

"What's up?"

"You are so good at manzai!"

"Hang on, that sounds good, but you're supposed to be saying the opposite of what you think."

"You never trip over your words, you're a handsome dude, you have a great voice and your family is rich—you're the best!"

"Uh-oh, this guy's getting annoying."

"You're a genius! A genius!"

"I'm going to slug you for that!" Yamashita yells at the top of his lungs.

The audience laughs and the walls seem to be laughing with them, giving back all the laughter they've absorbed from audiences who have sat here watching the comedy shows almost daily.

"But, dear partner! May I point out that even such a genius as yourself has some major faults."

"Like what?"

"For a start, your place is a pigsty."

"So my room is tidy...? Cheap ass! Can't you think of anything else?!"

"You eat like a bird and always take your time over meals."

"I eat like a pig and shovel it down...? Hey, you're making me look like an idiot!"

That part's true, actually. I can never eat at my own pace with Yamashita because he always finishes too fast.

"Your girlfriend is ugly."

"Very nice, but it's not about me!"

Yamashita's girlfriend is awesome, very sweet and classy.

"My partner has amazing talent!"

"Huh?"

"My talented, genius partner complained non-stop these last ten years, and couldn't keep up with me at all!"

I want to be a genius. I want to make people laugh.

"What are you saying?"

To everyone who doesn't like me, who I couldn't make laugh, I apologize.

"The last ten years have been hell because of you, no fun at all! I'm the unluckiest guy in the world!"

My partner made me into a manzai artist.

"And you, audience! How incredibly smart you are! You never pay a yen to come here every day and see comedians like us who've made it big and have a wonderful future ahead of us!"

The audience too has made me into a manzai artist.

"You're seriously smart. Thanks to you, every day was misery. Up yours!"

"Hey, no need for bad language!" Yamashita's face crumples.

"I never wanted to be a manzai comedian—even since I was a kid. It's the one thing I never ever wanted to do. Then I had the rotten luck to meet this guy in junior high and end up doing manzai. What a disaster!

It's killed me. This guy as good as murdered me! You murdering bastard!"

The audience is a blur, I can't see any more.

"Then sometimes, somebody comes along and praises us to the skies. That really makes our day. Isn't it wonderful when somebody tells you you're doing great? But then there are others who hate you! Who come along and throw cold water on all that sweet talk."

I scowl at the audience.

"When I hear you say Sparks suck! That you never want to see them again! That cuts me to the core. I hate your guts!"

I can hear sniffling in the audience. A mixture of laughter and tears. Kamiya is there, sitting at the back, crying the loudest of anyone.

"This is not the last time Sparks will ever perform manzai. When I think that I can see you every day from now on, I feel so happy. These last ten years have been a total waste for my future life. So I hope you all die the worst death!"

I'm performing as I always wanted to—yelling at the top of my voice, spit flying everywhere.

"Die! Die! Die! Die! Die! Die! Die! Die!"

I am totally in the moment, performing manzai with my partner. I turn to Yamashita. "Die!" I scream. "Die alone and away from your family!"

"Prick! Shut your mouth!"

Yamashita's voice has great delivery. And there's so much more manzai still to do... I wish I could keep doing it forever. Yamashita believed in me and let me lead. In return I gave him bitter, hard memories. I'm so sorry.

Yamashita's turn: "Listen! You spout abuse, you make the audience cry, you make your partner cry—how can you say that's manzai?! Manzai is supposed to make people laugh!"

"At last we did manzai that dumps on common sense."

"Put a sock in it!"

I never want this to end.

"Is there anything you'd like to say now we're nearly done?"

"Dear Partner! And audience! I am not grateful to you at all!"

Pause.

"You're a real schmuck, you know."

"You know, you just said the opposite too!"

Finally, genuine laughter from the audience.

"You really are good at manzai, aren't you?"

"We're done!"

We take a deep bow. The applause is endless.

The Net news that day carried an article with the headline "Sparks Break Up". My mother saw it too and sent me a message that said *Good work*. Over the last ten years I'd only ever told my parents the good things about my work. They'd helped me to become a manzai comedian too. I'd show my gratitude from now on if it killed me. I opened up the comments column for the article.

Who?!

No clue. Too many comedians!

Why do we need to hear about some lame act breaking up?

Saw them on TV but they were so boring they soon disappeared. Should try harder!

How many people have heard of them? Not me!

Comedians with no talent are not entertainers.

They're not funny. Where are all the good manzai comedians now, like there used to be?

It's an old photo. Maybe it's the only one of them.

Sorry. I only remember the silver hair.

They should've broken up sooner.

I'm an amateur but I'm still funnier than them.

I liked Sparks's manzai.

They're local amateurs, right? Anyone can be a comedian these days.

The dyed hair is a cheap stunt. Punks!

Thanks for the hard work (who?)

Great they got on Net news at the last.

Why bother writing who? etc.! Saw other responses
  like that but it's OK in relation to these two. Yeah. I
  don't know them either.
Who are they?! How come they're news?
Young comedians these days are simply not funny.
They don't train so no wonder they get dumped.

I was grateful for the few positive comments. They saved me. I was sorry about the negative opinions towards Sparks and all young comedians. Sorry that we hadn't been able to make people laugh. Sadly, we hadn't been able to sustain their fantasy that comedians are always funny.

I'd wanted to be a manzai comedian ever since I was a kid. If I hadn't met my partner in junior high, maybe it wouldn't have happened. I wasn't blaming anyone in particular for my not being able to make a living as a comedian, and I wasn't blaming it on the times or the economy either. In the public's eyes maybe we had achieved nothing more than becoming second-rate comedians. But to anyone who thinks they're funnier than me, I say this: Try getting up onstage yourself, just once. I don't mean to sound superior, but see what it feels like when your view of the world is stripped naked. I want you to know the fear that no one will laugh at the jokes you thought up—or the thrill when people do laugh.

It takes guts to keep working for a long time at something that nobody thinks essential. Especially when you think how you only get one chance at life—the thought of putting your heart and soul into something that might not produce results is scary. But avoiding risk isn't the answer. Doesn't matter whether they're chicken-hearted, deluded or hopeless fools. Only those who can stand on the stage—and take all the risks—and put *everything* they have into breaking down the barriers of common sense, can be manzai artists. I'm glad I understood that at least. It might've been a wild dream, but spending these ten years on giving it a shot meant that I got to own my life.

We hadn't been to Mifune in Harmonica Alley for a long time. I felt nostalgia at the sight of the steep stairs leading to the upper floor. It was crowded up there. The beckoning cat figurine was next to the small TV the same as always. Kamiya sat opposite me, poking at a plate of fried pork and garlic stems, and drinking shochu on the rocks.

"That was a hell of a performance," Kamiya said without irony. He looked happy at the thought, then drained his shochu in one gulp.

"I saw you crying," I said, smiling at the memory.

"Yeah, I was crying. Never seen manzai like it. The logic, the explosion of emotion... Two contradictory elements brought together like that. Sparks really nailed it." Kamiya avoided looking at me, his voice was thick.

"Nobody laughed. But if you say we did good, that makes me happier than anything." I honestly felt that.

From the very first sip of drink, Kamiya had done nothing but praise me. The cheap food at this place was comforting, just like it used to be.

"Kamiya, I'm sorry."

He kept on eating the food with gusto and gave no reply. I wanted to know what he thought about me quitting manzai. After all, Kamiya had declared he would be a manzai artist from the day he was born to the day he died, and it probably never even entered his head I might quit the business because Sparks had broken up. Kamiya had been my sensei, the person who'd taken most care of me—I had to tell him, even if he was disappointed. I couldn't run away from it.

"I don't know what I'll do next, but I decided to quit comedy," I said.

"Oh."

He was giving me this tender look. I was glad the restaurant was noisy.

"You already decided?"

"Yeah. Yamashita's the only partner for me. When he decided to quit, that was it for me too. Just the way it is."

I always was a sucker for Kamiya when he spoke kindly. After spending all that intense time hanging out together day after day, he's the one who made me into the comedian I became. I felt fortunate to have met him. But I had no regrets about deciding to leave comedy without consulting him first. I'd stopped feeling guilty about things. Thanks to Kamiya I'd given up trying to speak fast. From him, I learned to be myself. He'd given me a very human, passionate and practical demonstration of a lesson so simple and obvious you might see it written on a poster tacked to the wall of a pub toilet. But very soon, I had to separate from Kamiya and make my own way in life.

"Tokunaga." Kamiya swallowed a mouthful of pork and looked up.

"Yes," I said, trying for the right tone.

"There's no retirement for me. But you, Tokunaga, spent ten years thinking up gags and kept people laughing in their seats all that time." Kamiya's expression was mild, but his voice was steely.

"But there were days when no one laughed."

"There were. But you kept trying. Because you have acquired an incredibly specialized skill, like a boxer's punch. Even unknown boxers can kill someone with their punch. Comedians are the same. The difference is the more we punch the happier we make people. So even if you quit the agency and make your living from other work, you still have the ability to knock people out with laughter. There's no one else, anywhere, with a punch like yours."

I couldn't believe Kamiya was using a boxing metaphor. "Knock people out with laughter." Was that cool or not cool?

But he was on a roll: "You can't do manzai by yourself. You need at least two people. I can't do it even with two. Sometimes I wonder if I would have tried so hard if I was the only manzai artist in the world? We got where we are only because we're surrounded by people, amazing people, who somehow crazily share our vision. And we start thinking about what they haven't done, or continuing what they started. It's, like, a collaboration."

Where was he going with this?

"Only a couple in each generation make it big, manage to make a mark. But you get compared, you come up with your own stuff and maybe you get knocked out along the way. It's a big, terrible frigging contest, with winners and losers. But that's why it's interesting. Do we ever quit because we're scared? The losers that get eliminated, they were never a waste. Maybe some of them wished they'd never tried in the first place—regret is powerful shit—but I bet most, even those who never scored, who maybe weren't any good, don't have regrets.

It'd be piss-ass boring if there was only one duo in town. Everyone is necessary—even the ones who only ever go onstage once. And every comedian has people behind them, supporting them and making them into comedians just by being there. Lovers, friends or family."

For me it was Yamashita, and Kamiya, and my family, and kohai. And Maki, too. Anyone who ever touched my life helped make me into a manzai comedian.

"Abso-fucking-lutely every single person is necessary," Kamiya went on, stirring the ice in his glass with his little finger. "We're connected to all the manzai comedians yet to come. Which means, doesn't matter what you do: there's no retirement."

Kamiya looked embarrassed as he put the glass, which now contained only ice, to his lips.

"Thank you. Wherever I go, I'll knock 'em out with laughter," I said, with exaggerated emphasis on the laughter.

"You're taking the piss outa me," Kamiya said.

*　　*　　*

After quitting manzai I worked non-stop at two pubs to make a living. Yamashita went back to Osaka and got a job in a mobile phone store. Occasionally I contacted

Kamiya. By now I had over twenty notebooks for his biography. More than half was about myself and Sparks and musings of the heart. But I thought if I put together all the anecdotes I had about Kamiya, I probably had enough for a biography.

Problem was I still didn't know how to write a biography and hadn't read a single one. I had the poems Kamiya had written that he said I absolutely had to put in, but wondered if it was OK to put that kind of thing in a biography.

In late November, when the wind became so cold you knew winter was not far behind, I got a call from Obayashi asking if I knew Kamiya's whereabouts. He'd disappeared, and wasn't turning up for work. Supposedly he was in debt to the tune of some 10 million yen.

I tried calling Kamiya up straight away, but the line wouldn't connect. That same day I went to his apartment in Mishuku, where it was clear from the gas and electricity notices hanging on the doorknob that he wasn't living there any more. Maybe he was with Yuki in Sangenjaya, but if he was hiding out, I owed him the respect of letting him hide.

I walked back to Route 246 where a cold wind left me whipped and chilled. Several taxis went by in a row, all empty. The driver of each one slowed down to peer at me as they passed by, making me feel as if I were some animal being hunted by enormous monsters. Where the hell was Kamiya?

*   *   *

Eventually, through an acquaintance, I landed a job with an estate agency in Shimokitazawa. I wasn't much good at office work, but my experience in the entertainment business came in handy sometimes. Once, two young guys came to the office looking to rent an apartment. They were planning to move to Tokyo to try and break into comedy—and they actually recognized me, knew my work. As I showed them prospective apartments, they would say funny things and check my reaction. I was the perfect test audience for them, and I smiled throughout, but laughed only when they really did say something funny. They dazzled with their innocence and enthusiasm, proudly showing off each other's humour, so sure of their talent. I took them to a place near Wadabori Park, which was great for practising their routines.

Kamiya was still missing. There were rumours he'd been forced to appear in pornographic videos to pay off his debt, but I didn't believe that.

Then one evening, as I was sitting alone having a bowl of chicken giblet stew in Suzunari Alley in

Shimokitazawa, I got a phone call from an unknown number. Instinctively I knew it was Kamiya. "Wanna meet for a drink?" he asked with all casualness. I hadn't heard his voice for a year. Where would someone whose only interest is manzai go for a year? What had he been doing? I downed my glass of shochu, jumped into a taxi and headed for Ikejiri-Ohashi to a pub called Hana Shizuku near the station.

Kamiya was sitting in the back, where the light was turned down, and he waved me over. His face was already alcohol-red, and he was wearing a loose sweater with the sleeves rolled up, his jacket hanging over the back of the chair. He looked slightly thinner and wirier than when I last saw him. But something about him gave me a weird feeling. A sense of apprehension that something was badly off.

"Kamiya, where've you been the last year?"

My greeting sounded like a cross-examination.

"Heard you went looking for me. That was the word from Obayashi anyway. You know, that bastard slugged me," Kamiya said, pressing his hand gingerly against his cheek.

Obayashi had been pissed off, having to go around apologizing to everyone, but he did keep their registration at the agency while waiting for Kamiya to turn up.

OK, but what *was* this weird vibe I was getting?

"Tokunaga, listen to me. This sucks. I went to the agency to apologize today, but they said they didn't want me any more."

"Of course they wouldn't want you." There wasn't a job in the world you wouldn't get fired from if you went off for a year without a word, unless you had a damned good reason for it.

"I got into debt, deep deep debt, and there was no way out, so I went back to Osaka and ran around raising money."

"Did you pay it back?"

"In the end I declared bankruptcy and just paid off the people you shouldn't piss off if you value your life. Tokunaga, I tell you, stay out of debt. Debt collectors are like visitors from hell. They never leave you alone. This fuckhead, he left me phone messages, saying shit like, 'I'm on to you, you little prick. I know where you live—if you can call that living. Don't believe me? Check outside your door tomorrow. I'll leave you a little token of cigarette butts, same as you've been leaving around town. Don't fuck with me. Find some fucking cash.' So the next day I open my door and see this pile of cigarette butts. My stomach dropped. I was shitting myself. But the brand wasn't Short Hopes like I smoke, it was Menthol Pianissimo—a girl's smoke. I started yelling, 'Don't fuck with me!'"

Still, Kamiya looked happy enough chattering away, putting his spin on things. It was almost like old times—*almost*, because Kamiya seemed somehow very ill at ease.

"You know what, though? After I got some cash to give the jerk, we sorta became buds. He invites me to go play pachinko with him one night, but when I started losing, I had to borrow from him, and I couldn't pay it back, and he said I was shit after all, so every so often I get this friendly fucking call from him."

Why? Why was Kamiya so incapable of using the talents he was born with to make something of his life? How could he even be talking like this now?

It was at that moment it hit me. The thing I couldn't figure out, the thing that wasn't right. Kamiya had leant back in his chair, and what I saw gave me a major shock. In the eyes of the world of course, it was little more than a sideshow, a stupid gimmick, of no importance. But for me, it changed *everything*.

Kamiya then calmly removed his sweater to reveal two enormous breasts—if they could be called that.

The despair I'd managed to put away for so many years came to me again with arms wide open, greeting me with nostalgia and affection like an old friend.

"*What?!* Wh—what is that?!" I stared, unable to blink, unable to think.

"They're F cup," said Kamiya, his hands holding them up, showing them off.

I couldn't believe my eyes, my ears.

"What've you done?!" What the hell was he thinking?

"Well, if you're gonna do it, the bigger the better, eh? Go for the laughs. I got gallons of silicon pumped in."

Had he lost his mind?

"You know I always rejected the idea of personas, but then I thought, I don't need to. Something so funny it can't be defeated by a persona is totally funny, right?"

Seeing Kamiya go on so blithely about this left me with a mixture of... I don't know... fear, frustration, speechlessness. I cursed the world with all my heart.

"It won't work. The eyes go straight to those breasts. It's all you see. You don't see anything else. You don't hear anything."

I could hear how cold and cutting I sounded. From our first meeting, I knew Kamiya couldn't make a go of living like everyone else. Maybe it was none of my business, but all I wanted was for this guy, who always twisted things to the point of foolishness—if I could be forgiven for wishing something so banal—to simply be happy.

"Nobody's gonna laugh at that," I went on.

"Why not? It's funny."

"It's not funny. Not funny in the least. It's not a

persona, it's not anything. It's just bizarre, weird—off-the-charts weird. Do you think that's funny?"

Nobody understood him. Jeez, he was frustrating! All that talent wasted. Should I have just laughed at him?

"I thought I could get on TV with these." He looked at me with clear eyes.

"Hah, no way. Who's gonna laugh at an old guy in his thirties with huge breasts?"

Kamiya was an idiot. An utter lifelong fool.

"While I was getting them done, the whole time I thought how fucking hilarious it was. I couldn't stop laughing. But then I went to see someone afterwards, a salaryman friend—the only salaryman I know, matter of fact—and when I showed him and said I wanted to go on TV, he looked really turned off, like, disgusted, and that's when I got scared." Kamiya looked down.

"So then?" My voice was sharp.

"I got scared, thinking what have I done, but then I thought, Tokunaga will laugh."

"You thought I'd laugh at that?" I replied honestly, though I felt the prickle of tears. He was so vulnerable.

"Tokunaga, whaddya think? Don't you think I could get on TV?" Kamiya asked, looking me in the face, pleading.

I took a deep breath. "Kamiya," I began, "I know you didn't mean to be offensive. I say that because I've known you a long time. I think you did this because your sense of humour doesn't have normal bounds and you actually thought it'd be funny for a man to have gigantic breasts. But there's a lot of people out there who have a real-life hard time trying to work out stuff like their gender and sexuality and all that. Then you come along shaking those breasts? How do you think they're going to feel?"

These high-minded words coming out of my mouth were a surprise to me, but I made no effort to wipe away the tears that were beginning to roll down my cheeks. "Kamiya, I'm revolted." I barely managed to get those last words out.

Kamiya's eyes were wide open and red. Maybe I'd touched a nerve, I don't know. His shoulders heaved a little.

"You didn't do it to be nasty," I went on, "but people out there, people dealing with these matters, they have families and friends. If everyone was like you, crazy, no holds barred, maybe no problem. Or maybe if you did it because you wanted to be a woman, maybe no problem. But that's not how it was, right? The world knows, and we know, there are mean terrible fuckers who *do* make fun of people who aren't so-called normal, who have stuff to work out. Anyone who doesn't know you might think you're one of those fuckers. Because they don't have any other way of knowing you. They see your enormous breasts, they see you think it's a joke, they judge you by what they see. I know you, Kamiya. I know you have a heart. I know you're not one of those lousy fuckers. But public opinion counts. Ignoring public opinion is the same as being unkind. By definition, that's almost the same as being unfunny."

"Tokunaga, stop. Please don't say any more."

"I'm not accusing you."

"No, I'm bad. This was my bad. I'm a real fucking fool."

Crushed. Kamiya was on the verge of crying, taking care not to shake his breasts. "This is how it happened, Tokunaga. Apart from you, for years no one's said I was funny. The reason I never quit comedy is that you always said I was funny. I was always looking for a way to get across what I thought was funny. But those fuckers out there who decide who's funny, what's funny—they didn't get it. I wanted them to get it. I wanted them to say, 'That fool Kamiya is a gas—he's really funny.' I didn't know how to do it. Then, before I knew it, I had these tits. What the hell am I going to do with them? I'm so sorry."

A young couple sitting across from us were eating soba with such seriousness and manners they could have been having a last supper. At the biggest table in the room, a group of office workers were drinking noisily, keeping the waiting staff busy with their orders. The clamour coming from the kitchen, too, was a reminder of ongoing life.

Kamiya had never been able to blend into his surroundings. And once again I was there with him, in a space apart from everyone else, feeling wretched about the enormous breasts that were there too, and thinking back over the last ten years. In that moment, which felt like eternity, we sobbed our hearts out.

Kamiya was wearing an oversized jacket over a thick sweater to hide the swellings on his chest. We were on the Kodama bullet train, swaying along the tracks, en route to a hot spring for the New Year's holiday, a trip I had suggested to celebrate his birthday and to take a break. What I really wanted was to go to some tropical island, but since that was not an option, we were headed to Atami.

Kamiya was in high spirits, determinedly squeezing enjoyment out of every moment. Even though the train ride was less than an hour, he insisted on having a glass of shochu and opening up a packet of dried squid to go with it.

"Tokunaga, I'm sorry. It's gonna be weird for you going into the hot tub with me," he said.

"Oh, zip it," I replied.

"I don't even know whether to go into the men's side or the women's."

"The men's, of course."

"What if people freak out? You know how I hate causing trouble."

"But you're a genius at causing trouble."

In fact I'd anticipated trouble and planned ahead, booking us an expensive room with a private outdoor tub that had water from the hot spring piped directly into it. And I'd learned that at certain times of the day, the communal outdoor tubs could be reserved for private use.

When the train slid into Atami, Kamiya threw what was left of the dried squid into his mouth. He was still chewing on it when we reached the hotel.

Apparently, fireworks were held throughout the year in Atami, not only in summer, so in the evening we headed down to the seaside for the show. The corporate sponsors were announced over the loudspeaker before each round was launched, with one burst after another of fantastic fireworks lighting up the winter sky. Every explosion was greeted with applause and oohs and ahhs. We were having a great time.

After a particularly magnificent round of fireworks, there was a long pause during which everyone sat in a daze while white smoke drifted downward. Then the announcer's voice—a little nervous, a little more animated—came over the loudspeaker again: "Dearest Chie, you're the best. Let's get married." The crowd, not expecting anything like this, reacted with gasps of delight. As people turned to each other, a burst of fireworks was launched, but it was so lacklustre in comparison to the corporate extravaganza of what had come before, the contrast was ridiculous. It made me laugh out loud—this lesson on the harsh reality of the world, that you don't always get what you pay for when you put your heart into something. But in the next moment, I was drowned out by thunderous cheering, which built to a volume that exceeded even the boom of the fireworks. It was a collective attempt to congratulate the couple—also to save them from embarrassment. Kamiya and I joined in, clapping furiously until the palms of our cold hands turned red.

"How about that for human kindness, hey?" Kamiya said.

After the fireworks were over, we went to the same pub we'd gone to when we first met.

When the waitress came by to ask for our order, Kamiya looked up at her sentimentally. "You haven't changed a bit," he said. "We were here ten years ago. Remember us?"

"But I just started last month," she replied with a smile.

Kamiya was still in high spirits when we got back to the hotel. In the lobby he discovered that CDs were available on loan.

"Do you have anything by the Clash or the Sex Pistols?" he asked the receptionist in a monotone, thrown perhaps by how incredibly young she appeared.

"But you never listen to that stuff," I interjected.

"What would you know—I'm really into punk now," he said with a wild look.

We were out of luck. Most of the CDs had already been checked out, so we had to content ourselves with the leftovers.

"Strange how so many other punk fans are staying here tonight," Kamiya said drily.

Back in our room we ate and drank some more. Kamiya was excited, having seen a poster for an amateur comedy competition the next day. First prize was 100,000 yen. He was determined to enter and wouldn't listen to me telling him the deadline for entering had passed.

"I'm gonna work up some gags," he announced and went off, drink in hand, for a soak in the outdoor tub.

Once a comedian always a comedian, I thought as I opened up my Kamiya notebook and, as usual, started writing down the day's events.

"Oh, hell, it's the live version!" Kamiya yelled from outside. He must have been talking about the Bob Marley CD he'd just put on.

I looked up and saw a crescent moon floating high above Kamiya's head. A miracle of perfect, everyday beauty. Kamiya was here, simply, in this place. Alive and breathing, his heart beating. He was here. Body and soul, he gave himself to life, living it out on his own messy, irrepressible terms. As long as he was alive, there could be no bad ending. The two of us were still in mid-story. We would continue.

"Everything's gonna be alright," the hero of Jamaica kept singing to the world.

"Hey, I hit on a kick-ass gag," Kamiya shouted. He was standing there, stark naked against the night, gleefully shaking his beautiful breasts, bouncing them up and down, over and over.

JAPANESE FICTION
AVAILABLE AND COMING SOON
FROM PUSHKIN PRESS

MS ICE SANDWICH
Mieko Kawakami

SPARK
Naoki Matayoshi

MURDER IN THE AGE OF ENLIGHTENMENT
Ryunosuke Akutagawa

RECORD OF A NIGHT TOO BRIEF
Hiromi Kawakami

THE HONJIN MURDERS
Seishi Yokomizo

SPRING GARDEN
Tomoka Shibasaki

COIN LOCKER BABIES
Ryu Murakami

SLOW BOAT
Hideo Furukawa

THE HUNTING GUN
Yasushi Inoue

SALAD ANNIVERSARY
Machi Tawara

THE CAKE TREE IN THE RUINS
Akiyuki Nosaka